Seana jumped right into Ryan's arms

He cushioned the shock of her landing, then his arms locked firmly around her waist as he stared down at her. "Will you please let me go?" she said, struggling as her body began to respond to the warmth of him.

"No, I don't think so," he replied. "I'd just as soon hang on to you; this way I know exactly what kind of trouble you're likely to get into."

"No!" The cry escaped her lips only an instant before he claimed them with his mouth. She made herself rigid, but Ryan ignored her lack of response, kissing her lips, then running his own lips across her cheek, down her neck, back to nibble teasingly at her ear.

"You're just bound and determined to make things difficult for yourself, aren't you?" he whispered in her ear.

Battle of Wills

Victoria Gordon

Harlequin Books

TORONTO • NEW YORK • LOS ANGELES • LONDON
AMSTERDAM • PARIS • SYDNEY • HAMBURG
STOCKHOLM • ATHENS • TOKYO • MILAN

Original hardcover edition published in 1982
by Mills & Boon Limited

ISBN 0-373-02540-8

Harlequin Romance first edition April 1983

To Dana . . . and to Tom and Sharon,
wherever they are *this* summer.

Printed in U.S.A.

CHAPTER ONE

THE aged Volkswagen coughed once, consumptively, then gathered strength once more and burrowed its snout into the surge of the headwind it had been battling for the last sixty miles. Seana's reaction was less instant; she held her breath for nearly a minute, eyes locked on the approaching T-intersection as if she could draw herself and her vehicle there by sheer willpower.

She exhaled only when she halted at the intersection and found the car's engine still ticking over like a sick sewing machine.

Clairmont Corner. Only three, four miles at the most and she'd surely find a service station. Provided, of course, the old car didn't run out of gas first, she thought with a rueful twist of her lips. The headwind had taken a severe toll of the car's fuel range, and she'd been running on the reserve tank far too long already.

She sat for nearly five minutes, unable to make her turn because of the stream of oncoming traffic. And for every minute she seemed to hold her breath for most of it, ears pricked for the sound of the final, coughing death rattle that would mean a three- or four-mile walk.

Most of the traffic was large heavy trucks moving from the Grande Prairie oilfields, mobile giants that brooked no argument in their demands for right of way.

But finally she got a break, and stamping on the accelerator, Seana forced the car across the oncoming traffic lane and turned south for Grande Prairie and safety. She made the turn with room to spare, only to find herself with a brand-new driving problem; the headwind was now a vicious, erratic crosswind, a mischievous, unpredictable demon that toyed with her ageing car in a game that pushed her driving skills to their limit. The strong west wind would first shove at the car, bunting it towards the looming bulk of an oncoming truck; then with diabolical suddenness the wind would hold its breath, and Seana's own pull on the steering wheel would fling the small car to the right, where patches of spring snow still lay like streams of dirty cotton waste in the deep ditch.

'Oh, lord! I'd have been safer to run out of gas,' she muttered aloud; then instantly regretted it as the car took a final slurp from the reserve tank, coughed, and sagged into an almost uncontrollable lethargy.

'Oh . . . damn, damn, damn!' Seana moaned, stabbing furiously at the accelerator despite knowing it would do no good. She raised her left foot and then jammed it down on the clutch, eyes searching frantically for a wide spot where she could get the car out of the traffic lane.

Silent prayers and the car's own momentum were just enough to carry it the few metres necessary so that Seana could turn into a broad, grass-choked driveway to a roadside field.

Seconds later she was out of the car, the wind tearing fiendishly at her long black hair and combining with frustration to bring tears to her eyes. They were large, wide-spaced eyes, so deep a purple as to look almost black beneath her sooty eyelashes and vivid, fine-drawn and high-arched brows. She stood looking angrily into the wind for a moment, oblivious to its ruthless assault on her hair and the mischievous tugs that lifted her skirt much higher than she would normally have accepted.

She didn't even notice the high four-wheel-drive

pick-up truck that eased to a halt behind her, and the wind whipped away the driver's voice as he called to her. It wasn't until he gently touched her shoulder that Seana realised she wasn't alone. She turned with a cry of alarm, and as she faced him, the devilish wind called up a particularly vicious gust to launch her into his outstretched arms.

Her small shriek of dismay was muffled as her face was pushed into his chest, the crown of her head tucked beneath his chin to mingle with the rich, carrot fullness of his beard. For an instant her nostrils flared at the masculine scent of him, then strong hands grasped at her shoulders as he held her away from him and looked down into her eyes.

'I'm pleased you're so glad to see me,' he said, teeth glinting in a grin that was half teasing, half ... something else.

The voice emerged from a forest of moustache, beard and wind-blown, fiery hair, but it was his eyes that Seana noticed first. They were green, but a green so pale that at first she took them for grey. And they fairly blazed with intensity from a skin so sunburned it seemed like fine leather. Holding her still, his hands gently firm on her shoulders, the man stared almost mockingly into her own dark eyes, then carelessly ran his eyes down the length of her shapely figure before lifting them again to meet her indignant glance.

'We really *will* have to stop meeting like this,' he said then, grinning hugely as she pulled back in a futile attempt to escape his grip.

'I can stand up by myself,' she snapped, unwilling to make a scene by struggling too obviously, yet suddenly quite desperate to free herself.

'So I noticed,' he chuckled, blandly ignoring the hint. 'What's the matter with your beetle—run out of rubber bands?'

His mockery made her leap instinctively to the decrepit vehicle's defence. 'My car,' she said firmly, 'is apparently out of gas.'

This time when she shrugged against his grip, he released her instantly, then bared his teeth in a mocking laugh as the traitorous wind promptly thrust her back against him.

'Having trouble making up your mind, are you?' he grinned, but made no further attempt to restrain her as she once again lurched free.

In the process, Seana's eyes caught the time on his wrist-watch, and she quickly checked her own to confirm it. 'Oh, no!' she cried. 'I'm going to be late ... I just know it!' She turned then to face the man, her voice pleading. 'Look, I don't want to trouble you, but I've got an appointment in less than an hour. Could you please drive me to a service station or something? I've simply got to get some gas and get into Grande Prairie or I'll be late for my appointment, and ... and I just don't dare be late. I ... just can't!'

He shrugged. 'Do better than that, seeing you're in such a hurry. Get the lid open.'

The wind whipped at his words as he turned and walked to the rear of his truck and flung open the door of the home-made camper that crouched in the bed of the truck and extended over the cab as if resting on its elbows.

He moved, Seana noticed, with a long, loose stride, but his lean body seemed curiously contained, like some great cat in fluid motion. She wasn't aware of staring until he suddenly emerged from the camper, a ten-gallon drum of gasoline cradled in his arms. He stalked to the front of her car and set the drum down with a thud, shouting at her against the wind as he turned back to his truck.

'Well, don't just stand there; get the thing open. I

thought you were supposed to be in a hurry!'

Startled by the fierceness of his expression, Seana found herself scurrying to obey the command, but he'd already returned with a large screwdriver and a length of plastic hose before she could manipulate the lever which opened the hood of the car to give access to the gas tank. He stood watching, one eyebrow raised in obvious impatience, until she'd finally fumbled the latch open.

Then she stood by, feeling quite helpless and not a little embarrassed as he adroitly dropped to one knee and hoisted the drum on to the other—while he plopped one end of the hose in the drum and sucked on the other until he had a steady run of gasoline flowing. As the fuel flowed into the Volkswagen's tank, he spat distastefully several times, his eyes wincing and mouth writhing at the acrid taste of gasoline. But when he was finished, he dropped the near-empty drum and rose to his feet with a bright smile.

'There you are, ladybug. Just give me a minute and I'll be out of your way,' he said, hefting the drum and turning back towards his truck.

Ladybug? Seana's mind shifted quite irrelevantly to the old nursery rhyme, and she wondered if his use of the word might be some sort of omen reflecting on the interview she might now just be on time for. Then she was fumbling into her large handbag, seeking to get out some money as the red-bearded man returned to stop gracefully and pick up both the syphon hose and his screwdriver.

'I ... er ... I don't know how much to offer you,' she said lamely as he looked down at her with an amused glint in his pale green eyes.

'Don't worry about it for now. You can catch me later, when you're not in such a hurry,' he said.

'But ... but you don't even know me,' she stam-

mered. 'Please, I feel I must straighten this out now.'
Then she looked again at her watch. 'Oh, and if I don't
go now I'll still be late. Please, tell me how much.'

His laugh took on a note of careless harshness that
struck her pride like a thunderbolt. Then he moved
closer to stand with his face only inches from her own.

'Wasn't for the taste of the gasoline, I'd settle for a
kiss or two,' he said, voice like silk although his eyes
were hot with undisguised provocation. Then he
twisted his mouth in a grimace of distaste. 'But I
wouldn't wish this taste on anybody, so I'll settle for a
raincheck. You're going to be around G.P. for a
while?'

It wasn't really a question, but Seana felt conscience-
bound to answer. She met his glance, aware that they
were surrounded in an aura of physical awareness like
nothing she'd ever experienced before. 'I . . . I hope
so,' she said in a low voice, her stomach tightening as
his eyes burned into hers.

Then he shrugged, almost like a horse throwing off
flies, and the light in his eyes faded slightly. 'Okay,' he
said. 'Leave it for now.'

'But I can't,' she replied. 'I mean, if I get this job
. . . well, I won't exactly be . . . where we'd be able to
find each other. Please, let me pay you now.'

'Have you got a name, ladybug?' The question cut
across her protest, nullifying it almost rudely. .

'Seana. Seana Muldoon,' she replied, unable to resist
the command in his voice.

'And where will you be . . . presuming you get this
job you're almost certain to be late for?'

'I don't know.' The reply was totally honest, but at
the scowl it brought, she expanded somewhat. 'I'm
serious. I'm hoping to work in forestry, on a fire tower.
But I don't know where. They haven't told me anything. Oh . . . really, I simply *must* go now!'

'That's what I told you five minutes ago,' he chuckled. 'Now stop arguing, get in the car, and get to it. I don't want you blaming me for the fact if you turn up late.'

And to her amazement he turned away without so much as a farewell, waving one hand not in goodbye, but in a stern gesture to get her into her car and away.

Seana looked after him incredulously, then flung herself in a quick dash that allowed her to catch up only after he had clambered into his truck and slammed the door. She had to pound on the window to get him to notice her, and he opened it to smile down at her enquiringly.

'Are you still here?' he asked in mock amazement. 'I suppose now you've lost your car keys.'

'I have *not*,' she replied, feeling the first flush of real embarrassment but determined to follow through her original intention. 'I just . . . what's your name?'

'Does it matter?' His voice was deliberately soft now, his eyes alight with an unholy, teasing humour.

'Well, of course it matters,' Seana snapped. 'Do you think I'd deliberately make myself late if it didn't?'

'Gee, I don't know. Women do such strange things sometimes,' he replied tauntingly.

It was too much. Seana turned away before her mouth said something vicious, but her angry walk left no doubt as to her feelings. She was several paces from the truck when his voice forged through the wind to catch her.

'Hey!' She ignored him, but when he repeated the call she turned and glared at him, oblivious to the warmth of his smile as he finally answered her.

'Ryan,' he said, then churned the truck engine to life. 'Ryan Stranger.' And before she could reply he had slammed the vehicle into gear and slewed out on to the highway, one hand raised in a friendly yet mocking salute.

Ryan Stranger. Seana mouthed the name over and over as she got her own car going, sending it flying into town and thinking herself doubly lucky to find a parking spot handy to the Forestry Department offices.

An unusual name. And, she was forced to admit, an unusual man—exasperating, annoying, deliberately and blatantly antagonising. And yet nice. Also, she thought, very, very handsome, in his own way. Then as she scampered up the stairs towards the superintendent's office, she laughed aloud.

'Handsome! How could I tell?' she said half aloud. For all she knew, he could have any sort of face hidden beneath that incredible fiery beard. Maybe no chin at all, for instance. And yet she knew, somehow, that the portions of his face that the beard disguised were just as handsome as what had been revealed. There was simply no way that those piercing, pale green eyes, that aquiline nose and the broad, generous mouth could go with a weak chin or any other beard-hidden flaw.

But she forgot about Ryan Stranger when she pushed open the Forestry Department door and stepped inside with an unconscious glance at her wristwatch.

'You're just in time,' said a warm, welcoming voice, and Seana looked up to see a motherly, white-haired woman in her late fifties, smiling at her kindly. 'I'm Mrs Jorgensen,' the woman said, 'and you'll be Seana Muldoon, of course. Sit down, please. The super's expecting you, but he'll be a minute or two.'

Seana sat down gladly, grateful for the chance to catch her breath. But she was barely into her chair when the woman's next words brought her to startled alertness.

'Don't be . . . surprised if the interview doesn't go quite as you'd expected,' the older woman said. 'I think you'll find that the super—his name's Frank Hutton, by the way—might be just a wee bit surprised when he sees you.'

'I don't understand,' Seana replied. 'Why should he be surprised?'

'Let's just say you don't look quite as much like your father as I think he's expecting,' Mrs Jorgensen replied with a knowing grin.

Seana blanched. 'You mean . . .' Her question was aborted by a buzz from the intercom and a gruff voice that followed it.

'Mrs J.! If Muldoon's here, let's get on with it. The appointment was for eleven-thirty, wasn't it?'

'Coming in now, sir,' Mrs Jorgensen replied, waving Seana through the inter-office door with a good-luck gesture.

The man behind the desk didn't even look up as Seana walked briskly into the office, her upright carriage and posture hiding an uncertainty she dared not reveal. All she could really see of him was a stubble of close-cropped white hair as he studied some papers before him, blindly waving her to a seat opposite him.

She seated herself without a word and waited patiently as he continued the charade of ignoring her. It was only too obvious, she thought, that this man made it a habit to keep his subordinates thoroughly under his thumb.

Her father had been slightly inclined that way, so Seanna knew enough to restrain her urge to giggle when Frank Hutton muttered, 'Now, Muldoon,' and then looked up to see her for the first time. He stifled a half-uttered oath, then demanded, 'Who the hell are you?'

'Seana Muldoon, sir,' she replied with a perfectly

straight face which she slowly softened to a light smile.
'I'm here about the tower job.'

'I know very well why you're here,' he snapped, the
blustery answer revealing the obvious confusion he felt
as he shuffled through the papers once more, this time
emerging with the file of letters she had written in ap-
plication. He slowly scanned the signature of each
letter before looking up at her again with an obvious
mixture of confusion and genuine embarrassment.

'Well,' he finally said with a shrug of snowy eye-
brows, 'I guess it's my mistake after all, Miss
Muldoon. And one I must certainly apologise for, since
I truly had no intention of wasting both your time and
my own by letting this thing go so far . . .'

His voice trailed off hopefully, but Seana was too
wise to grab at the proffered bait. She settled back
demurely in her chair, throttling the anger that
seethed inside her, and determined to force Frank
Hutton to handle the problem the hardest possible
way—if at all.

There was a lengthy pause as they surveyed each
other across the broad desk. Frank Hutton made no
attempt to disguise either his impatience or his discomfort; Seana did her absolute best to exude a calm
attitude. It was the man who finally broke the silence.

'Really, I feel quite bad about this,' he said, again
pausing hopefully to wait for a response. Seana stayed
put.

And when the white-haired superintendent finally
resumed the conversation, it was with the air of a man
trapped by desperation but determined to see things
through.

'I'm sure you can understand, Miss Muldoon, that
if I had realised you were a . . . a woman, this would
never have gone to this point. I mean, I simply cannot
take the responsibility for putting a young, and if I

may say so, very attractive young woman out on one of those isolated forestry towers by herself.'

Again there was that hopeful pause, and Seana found herself facing the growing certainty that he wanted *her* to say the right words to bail him out of the situation. But despite her growing anger, a seething, white-hot fury that threatened to erupt momentarily, she spoke out finally in a voice placid with false calm.

She fell back on the ploy once taught her by a university professor, perhaps the single best advice she had gained while seeking her zoology degree.

'It's a tough old world out there,' he had told his class. 'And you'll find yourself back into a corner far more often than you'd expect. You'll find all kinds of people trying to put words in your mouth and trying to make you accept them as gospel, no matter what they're trying to promote. Don't! One of the fastest ways to stop that sort of thing is just to sit back and ask only one thing—*why*? By the time they're through answering that question, you'll have all the time you need to formulate your own ideas on the subject and make sure the words in your mouth are your own.'

It was a trick Seana had found useful, particularly with less professional instructors, but never before in her young life had so much hung in the balance. Still, she hesitated only fractionally before demanding in what she hoped was a firm but rational tone, 'Why?'

The effect was nothing short of miraculous. Frank Hutton's jaw quite literally dropped, then clamped shut again so firmly there were angry lines in his face. Instead of answering immediately, he stabbed at the intercom and growled, 'Is he here yet?'

There was no reply, but a second later the office door opened to admit the tall, cat-like figure of . . . Ryan Stranger.

There was no opportunity for either of them to utter

greetings, or even really to acknowledge each other's presence. Frank Hutton didn't greet Ryan Stranger either; he bluntly demanded: 'Can you give me three good reasons why I should let this woman manage White Mountain Tower this summer?'

Seana sat bolt upright in her seat. What a loaded, deliberately treacherous question! she thought, and glared at Ryan Stranger as if it were his fault. He returned her glance silently, appraisingly, and although it might have appeared like idle curiosity to Frank Hutton, Seana's own reactions told her it was more than an idle appraisal. This lean, arrogant, red-bearded devil was undressing her with each sweep of his eyes.

She wanted to look away, but couldn't. She had to force herself to meet those horrid pale green eyes, but she did it. Until suddenly, without warning, he replied to Frank Hutton's question without so much as verbally acknowledging Seana's interest in the discussion.

'I could give you a dozen reasons why you shouldn't,' he said, 'but I don't think I can answer the question the way you asked it.'

Seana knew her mouth must be hanging open, but as the fury leaped to her eyes, she was oblivious to her appearance. 'You . . . you . . .' she spluttered, unable to find words, to untwist her tongue, to say anything coherent at all. Her mind was lucid enough, but she couldn't link it to her tongue, and by the time she thought it possible, Frank Hutton's answer had her reeling in total confusion.

'That's a bit rough, Ryan,' the white-haired man was saying. 'I mean, I've already given her the damned job. Don't you think she at least deserves a chance?'

Ryan Stranger shrugged. 'Not at White Mountain Tower,' he said. 'Damn it, Frank, you know I'm planning to spend the summer up in that area. How the hell am I going to get anything done if I have to spend all my time nursemaiding a woman?'

As the forestry superintendent replied, Seana felt like some puppet-like observer. Her head kept snapping from one speaker to the other, her mind incapable of assimilating what she heard.

'You'd hardly have to nursemaid her,' said Hutton. 'She was practically raised on a tower, this girl. Damn it, man, she's Mike Muldoon's daughter!'

'I don't care whose daughter she is,' Ryan Stranger snapped. 'A forestry tower's no place for a woman unless she's too damned old and ugly to be anywhere else.'

'You're nothing but a chauvinist,' replied the forestry man, the same man Seana would have faced with an identical charge only moments before. There've been women on the towers for years. Hell, there was a woman on Bald Mountain Tower way back . . . back when Seana's dad was a ranger at Grovedale.'

Ryan Stranger's tone was implacable. 'Look, Frank, you asked for my opinion and I'm giving it to you. If you want this girl on a tower, be my guest. Put her on Copton Tower, or Kakwa, or any damned tower in Alberta *except* White Mountain. I've got too much to do this summer to be worrying about taking care of *her*.'

Seana's unrestrainable roar of rage halted any attempt at a reply by the superintendent.

'Stop! Stop it this very minute!' she cried angrily. 'I don't know which of you decided that I need a . . . a nursemaid, but you can just forget it. I'm perfectly capable of taking care of myself.'

She would have continued, oblivious to the fact that she was close to tears and her face was white with an anger that might totally erupt at any instant, but Ryan Stranger shook one huge fist at her, a gesture so unexpected it halted Seana as abruptly as if he had actually struck her.

'Yes, we know about that, don't we?' he said in a

soft, menacing tone. Then he rose lithely to his feet and stalked cat-footed to the door, where he turned for a final word to Frank Hutton. 'You please yourself on this one, Frank. But if you're smart you'll take my advice.'

He was through the door, closing it softly and yet angrily behind him, before either of the room's remaining occupants could reply.

'Well, that was a bit much,' Frank Hutton finally remarked. 'I'm ... surprised at Ryan, although I'm damned if I know why I should be. And I'm sorry to have put you in such a hot seat, Miss Muldoon. I really don't know how to make it up to you, except to say that of course you have the job.'

Seana could barely reply; so firm a hold had her anger that she was almost afraid to open her mouth. The absolute nerve of Ryan Stranger! And the audacity! How *dared* he say such things on the basis of a single incident?

'Well, I'm certainly pleased at that,' she finally managed to say. But her mind wasn't on the job; she was thinking only of Ryan Stranger and how thoroughly, hatefully nasty he'd been.

'No question of it,' Frank Hutton said. 'Actually, I'd invited Ryan to drop by so you two could meet. Or rather so he could meet *Sean* Muldoon, as I honestly thought of you. Since you'll both be working in the same area, I thought it best to have the ... er ... formal introductions in a sort of ... official situation, if you get what I mean. Save any possible problems later with regard to responsibility and authority ...'

'I gather you're trying to say that Ryan Stranger is inclined to be a bit heavyhanded in his dealings,' Seana retorted. 'Yes, I think I've got the message. He's a regular little dictator, isn't he? Well, don't worry about that aspect of things; I'm quite certain I'll be able to handle Mr Stranger without any trouble at all—not that I expect I'll be seeing much of him now in any event.'

'Don't be too sure,' replied her new boss. 'He's pretty hot-tempered, but it never lasts long. He'll turn up sooner or later, you can bet on it. Just remember, Seana, that White Mountain Tower will be *your* tower; you're in charge and you're responsible. If Ryan does try to pull anything that seems ... er ... irregular, you've only to get on the radio and somebody will be out to set him straight.'

Seana shrugged her shoulders to disguise the tremor that fluttered through her slender body. It would be folly to let Hutton realise that she wasn't really that confident in her ability to handle Ryan Stranger, and yet ...

'You're certain you wouldn't rather put me on another tower? I mean, I wouldn't want to be responsible for causing trouble between you or anything,' she ventured.

'Hah! Ryan Stranger can cause quite enough trouble on his own,' Frank Hutton snorted. 'No, it's White Mountain Tower for you, and if Ryan doesn't like it he can put it someplace uncomfortable. Can you be ready to go in the morning?'

So soon? And yet, Seana wondered, what else should she have expected? It was spring; the grass was drying despite the tendrils of late snow in the shady places. Farmers would be starting to do their spring burning, one of the worst hazards for a forest surrounded by settlement.

'Yes, I suppose so,' she replied, not really sure but unable to think of a good reason not to start the next day. At the very least it would mean less of a hole in her small financial nest-egg.

'Good,' he said, rising to shake her hand. 'Welcome

to the Alberta Forest Service, Seana. I'll have Mrs J. make all the arrangements this afternoon, and first thing tomorrow we'll get you loaded and on your way.'

He ushered Seana from his office, apparently unaware that she moved almost as if in a daze, and turned her over to Mrs Jorgensen with a brief list of instructions about food, water, schedules and equipment.

'My goodness, child, you look absolutely exhausted!' the older woman exclaimed as soon as Frank Hutton was safely back in his office. 'I suppose you drove all the way from Edmonton this morning, too. Have you very much to arrange before you leave tomorrow? It'll be your last chance for some time.'

'No, I've got nothing at all to organise, really,' Seana replied dully. 'Except ... oh, it doesn't matter anyway.' She sagged wearily into a seat opposite Mrs Jorgensen.

'Well, with six hours of driving behind you, I suppose you've not had time to arrange anywhere to stay tonight,' the woman said. Without waiting for a reply, she rummaged into her purse and hefted an enormous key-ring before detaching one key, then wrote something on a scrap of paper and handed both to Seana.

'Here's my address, and this is the key to the back door,' she said. 'Why don't you go straight there, grab a shower and have a good long nap. I'll be home about four-thirty and we can plan a nice, leisurely meal and then send you off in the morning with a proper breakfast and a good night's sleep behind you.'

Seana tried to argue, but Mrs Jorgensen waved aside her objections as being of no consequence whatsoever.

'Nonsense, my child. I've lived alone these past three years—since my Tom died—and I'd be the first to admit I don't think much of it. I'd more than welcome the company and you look as if you need the sleep. Now be off with you; I've work to do if we're going to have you properly equipped for tomorrow.'

Seana found the large old house without difficulty, and in keeping with a last-minute directive from her hostess, parked the car in one half of the empty double garage. She took her purse and battered old suitcase with her and found her way to the back door.

Inside, the house had a slightly cluttered but homey look; it was clear Mrs Jorgensen couldn't ever be termed houseproud. A brief tour sufficed to find Seana the spare bedroom, and she quickly deposited her belongings before idly wandering through the rest of the house.

The living room yielded considerable information about its occupant. Family portraits hung in convenient places, intermingled with oil paintings of vivid, mountainous scenes and landscape studies. The furniture was heavy, old-fashioned but comfortable, and had obviously seen a lot of use over many years.

She roamed the kitchen to discover Mrs Jorgensen's obvious love of cooking. It was large, beautifully planned from the viewpoint of a working cook, and displayed many unusual cooking utensils hung from the walls and cupboards.

There were a few dishes in the sink, obviously from Mrs Jorgensen's breakfast that morning, and without really thinking about it Seana set about washing, drying and putting them away. She gazed idly out the window into the well-treed back yard as she did so, but her mind was seeing only the incredible chain of events that had occurred that day. She was still thinking about that when she finished the dishes, took a quick shower and lay down on the soft feather quilt in the guest room.

It was like a silent movie as the scenes flickered behind her closed eyelids—the steep hillsides of Smoky River Crossing, the tortured advance of her car against the headwind, the masses of traffic at Clairmont Corner. And then a new set of scenes, the lithe, catlike movements of Ryan Stranger, the cold but fiery gleam in his pale eyes, the very clothes he wore, so familiar to memory but unexpected in the modern world. Faded jeans and a woollen shirt beneath a scarlet bush vest, beaded Indian moccasins peeping from the moccasin rubbers on his feet, the fire of sunlight on his beard . . .

A breeze filtered through the half-open window, so Seana reached down to pull the eiderdown over her, luxuriating in the warmth and wondering idly if her own new sleeping bag would provide such comforts on White Mountain Tower. Then her mind drifted again, recounting Ryan's assistance that morning, contrasting it to his angry, unexpected attitude later in the day. It made no sense.

She deliberately closed her eyes more tightly, trying to blank out the mental pictures that sprang unbidden to her sleepy mind. It was a gesture wasted; all she did was intensify the image of Ryan Stranger's face, bringing it into clearer focus as he himself had done when he had stared down into her eyes by the roadside.

Damn the man anyway, Seana thought. And to think that she was still indebted to him! No matter his rude and quite inexplicable behaviour in Frank Hutton's office; he'd helped her and given her gasoline, and she would—must—find some way to repay him. And soon!

'I'll do it, too,' she said aloud, sitting upright in the bed with her eyes suddenly wide open. 'And I'll be damned and double-damned if it'll be the kind of repayment he expects!'

And yet, when she closed her eyes again, the thought of Ryan Stranger taking his payment in a kiss seemed far less disagreeable than it ought. Until sh forced herself to remember his actions in Frank Hutton's office, the way he had ridiculed her, deliberately tried to keep her from the job she so desperately wanted.

Insufferable chauvinist! she thought. How totally unfair to turn completely against her because of one single, isolated incident. Was it her fault the winds had been so strong? No. Nor was it her fault that Frank Hutton had decided she would be located at White Mountain Tower, but somehow she felt sure Ryan Stranger would blame her for it.

Finally she drifted into proper sleep, but even then the tall, lean, swaggering figure stalked through her dreams, pale eyes alight with mischief, muscular fingers reaching out to grip her shoulders, sensuous mouth twisted into a sneer that bespoke desire and yet rejected her.

She woke to the tinkling sound of Mrs Jorgensen setting the dining room table, and when she opened the bedroom door it was to the delicious smell of a pork roast nearing readiness in the oven. Surprised, Seana looked at her wrist-watch and nearly fainted. It was a quarter past seven!

'Oh, how could you let me sleep so long?' she exclaimed upon entering the dining room to find the table set and Mrs Jorgensen setting out a chilled bottle of wine in a cooler.

'I figured you'd sleep as long as you needed to,' was the reply. 'That drive up from Edmonton is a killer if you're not used to long-haul driving, and I'd suspect you're not. Besides, from the look of your eyes you *did* need the sleep.'

'You're right,' Seana admitted. 'But you certainly should have got me to help with this. It's not fair that you've worked all day and then had to spend hours preparing dinner as well. Not while I was busy sleeping my head off.'

'Fiddle-faddle,' Mrs Jorgensen replied. 'Besides, it looks as if you've done your share already. I don't usually leave my breakfast dishes like that, either, I'll have you know, but this morning I was in a bit of a hurry.'

Mrs Jorgensen moved towards the kitchen as she spoke, leaving Seana little choice but to follow, and it wasn't until they were through the doorway that Seana realised the table was set not for two—but for four.

She was about to ask about it when her hostess began talking about something quite different, and before Seana had a chance to ask, the other woman changed the subject yet again.

'Right, half an hour to go,' she announced briskly. 'I'm off to change in a minute, but before I go, may I ask if you've brought along anything . . . er . . . sort of dressed-up casual to change into? I suppose not, seeing there's not much call for fancy clothes at the tower. Hmm . . . best you come with me and we'll see what we can find.'

'But won't what I'm wearing be suitable?' Seana asked, 'or have you somebody special coming? Oh, dear, I feel I'm really in the way. You should have said something.'

'Nonsense—it's because of you that I've invited our guests,' was the reply. 'Now come along. I've got a light caftan that should be just right for you. You'll have all you want of jeans and T-shirts before the summer's out, my child. Tonight you're going to celebrate your new job in style.'

And style it was! The 'light caftan' was actually a flowing dream of soft mauves and lilacs that fitted Seana perfectly and suited her colouring even more perfectly. Much more suitable, they both decided, than her rather severe job interview outfit.

'It's ideal,' declared her hostess. 'In fact, after seeing it on you, Seana, I don't think I could ever do it justice again. So consider it a welcoming present and wear it in good health.'

'Oh, but I couldn't,' Seana protested, only to have her objections brushed aside with casual disdain.

'You can and you will,' said Mrs Jorgensen in tones that brooked no argument. 'Now hustle yourself out and pour us a small drink. I'll only be a few moments.'

Seana obeyed with a shake of her head, and when Mrs Jorgensen joined her in the living room a few minutes later, she raised her glass in salute and offered a genuine thanks for the hospitality and the gift.

Then both women adjourned to supervise the final meal preparations, mostly involving the creation of some home-made apple-sauce to go with the roast. Mrs Jorgensen was busy at that when the doorbell rang, so it fell to Seana to answer it.

She walked to the door in a sudden shroud of apprehension, a feeling so unexpected and yet so real that she wondered about it, suddenly tense and wary. As she reached out to open the door, it swung wide before her, revealing two figures on the porch.

One was an enormously tall, husky young man, but it was the other man who drew Seana's eyes and whose mere presence had her tongue-tied with surprise and shock.

CHAPTER TWO

'Hi there, ladybug,' said Ryan Stranger, his mouth twisted in a sardonic grin and one eyebrow raised in a gesture that fairly screamed out his amusement at Seana's surprise.

Worse, he seemed quite oblivious to the earlier events of the day and the effect they might be expected to have on whatever welcome he expected.

'Well, aren't you going to invite us in?' he went on, adding to her discomfort the knowledge that she'd been standing there in numbed silence for far too long.

But she couldn't, simply *couldn't* speak. Instead, she stepped silently to one side and waved the men forward with her hand, then closed the door behind them and meekly accepted the bottles of wine they thrust at her.

Mrs Jorgensen, thank goodness, chose that moment to enter the living room, and both young men shouted, 'Hullo, Mother,' almost in unison and lifted the white-haired woman clean off the floor as they planted smacking kisses on her rosy cheeks.

'Get down, you young fools!' she scolded with mock anger. 'You'll have the young lady thinking you've no manners at all.'

'Hah!' cried Ryan. 'She already thinks that of *me*. And probably worse, too.' Whereupon he turned to Seana, gesturing towards his enormous companion. 'This, by the way, is Ralph Beatty,' he said. 'And he's much better mannered than I am, I promise. Ralph—Seana Muldoon.'

The tall giant acknowledged the introduction with a

slow, almost shy nod and an even shyer smile. It was from Mrs Jorgensen that she received the information that Ralph was the chief resident fish and wildlife officer.

'You know where things are, Ryan,' the older woman said then. 'Pour yourselves a drink while Seana and I finish up in the kitchen, and we'll start dinner fairly soon. You might give us each a fresh sherry, too, if you wouldn't mind.'

Thankfully, she waited until the two women were alone in the kitchen before uttering her next remark. 'What's with you and Ryan?' she demanded without preamble. 'Lord, child, don't tell me you've fallen for him already? You've hardly been here a day!'

Seana suppressed a shudder. 'Nothing like that,' she replied grimly. 'Just the opposite, if you must know.'

'Heaven help us,' was the reply. 'That kind of reaction is even more dangerous than the other!'

Seana laughed, but it was a hollow, almost bitter laugh that fooled no one. Why, she wondered, had Mrs Jorgensen invited Ryan Stranger to a dinner supposedly in Seana's honour? Surely she'd heard his vitriolic remarks in the office, and if she didn't already know about Seana's initial encounter with the red-bearded tyrant, it would almost certainly come out at dinner.

She returned to the living room on the other woman's heels, unable to quell the rising apprehension inside her.

Ryan was waiting for her, her glass of sherry dwarfed in his fingers. But it was his eyes that compelled her attention, eyes that seemed to reach out and touch her, caress her; eyes like those of some great, predatory animal.

He had changed for dinner, of course, and the switch from rough bush clothing to a perfectly-cut three-piece suit was really quite astonishing in its effects. When she had first met him, Seana had reckoned him in his late twenties, but now she had to revise her estimate considerably. Thirty-five, she thought. Perhaps even closer to forty.

She also had to revise her estimate of his attractiveness. With his hair and beard combed, and dressed as he was, handsome became too tame a word. He wasn't, in any event, conventionally handsome. There was too much harshness, too many planes and angles in his features. And all of it dominated by those eyes . . .

'You just window-shopping, or do you want to buy?' he asked quietly, and Seana flinched with embarrassment at having been caught staring. Mrs Jorgensen and Ralph Beatty were already seated on the chesterfield, chatting comfortably and almost out of earshot.

'Neither, thank you,' she snapped. 'In fact, I can't think of anything less enticing.'

'Oh, prickly,' he replied with a mocking smile. 'Funny, I wouldn't have thought you'd be so temperamental.'

'Obviously,' she retorted, shifting to one side in a bid to get past him and join the others. He countered the move so easily she might have saved herself the effort.

'If I didn't know better, I'd think you'd taken a distinct dislike to me,' he said with that same, smirking grin. 'Really, Seana, have you no sense of humour, not to mention, of course, a sense of gratitude?'

'Oh!' she choked. How typical of this arrogant devil to remind her of her debt. No mention, of course, about how he'd gone out of his way to try and keep her from getting her forestry tower job, no mention of the insults heaped on her in front of a prospective boss. 'You're . . . despicable!' she retorted angrily.

'But loveable,' he replied without apparent offence.

'Mind you, there are those who wouldn't agree, but I think you'll find out in time that I am.'

'With any luck I won't ever have to find out,' she replied coldly. 'Especially in view of your comments in the forestry office.'

Exactly what she'd expected that remark to produce, she wasn't sure. But certainly it wasn't the howl of genuine laughter that brought instant silence from the room's other occupants.

'Now that's gratitude for you,' Ryan Stranger said to no one in particular. 'I save the lady's job for her and all she can do is abuse me!'

And to Seana's astonishment, both Mrs Jorgensen and Ryan broke into peals of honest laughter that was quickly joined by a chuckle from Ralph Beatty.

She looked from one to the other and back again, unable to figure out what could possibly be so funny, and when she returned her gaze to Ryan, he reached out unexpectedly to tuck one finger beneath her chin and grin down at her with the fond patience of somebody gentling a fractious child.

'You're astonishing, ladybug,' he laughed. 'I didn't think they made girls that naïve any more. You really were taken in by that performance today, weren't you?'

Unsure of his meaning, but decidedly not amused at apparently being made the butt of some private joke, she could only stare daggers at him, which seemed only to heighten his amusement.

It was left to Mrs Jorgensen to explain. 'But I thought you must have realised it was all an act,' she said between intermittent fits of the giggles. 'And a very well performed one at that, if *you* were taken in along with Frank Hutton.'

It wasn't, however, until they had gone in to dinner that the full details of the elaborate charade were explained to Seana. And by this time she was beginning to at least see some of the logic, if not the humour.

'Old Frank doesn't much like me,' Ryan explained, 'but he likes having women on his towers even less, as a general rule. So when Mrs J. realised that he didn't even know you were female until today, she and I reckoned we'd best do something to keep him from talking you out of the job.'

'Thank heaven for two-way intercoms,' Mrs Jorgensen added. 'I hate to think what might have happened if I hadn't been able to let Ryan listen in on what approach Frank was taking.'

'You mean you . . .' Seana was honestly shocked, despite the benefits she'd gained from the exercise.

'No, she didn't,' Ryan interjected. 'I did! And just be thankful, young lady, because one hint about my true thoughts on the matter of you going to White Mountain Tower and you'd be back on the road to Edmonton right now.'

He grinned then at her look of surprise. 'No kidding. And if I do say so, it was a sterling performance considering we only had about two minutes to get it together.' And he laughed. 'Poor old Frank! I wonder if he'll ever realise how easy he is to lead down the proverbial garden path.'

'Yes, well, I wouldn't go making too much of a habit of it,' said Mrs Jorgensen. 'You're already high enough in his bad books as it is. Let him just once realise how he's been taken in today, Ryan Stranger, and he'll have you barred from every tower site in the district.'

'And I certainly wouldn't want that to happen,' he said, looking at Seana in a glance that was startlingly meaningful. 'No sense going to all this trouble if I'm not going to be allowed to take advantage of it.'

Seana tried to meet his eyes directly, but there was a flame of attraction there she dared not meet, lest she be drawn to it like a moth . . . and perish.

The last thing she needed, she thought, was any kind of involvement with a man as frankly devious and cunning as Ryan Stranger. He was, Seana decided, much too fast on his feet for her liking, and much too aware of his attractive charm.

Her suspicions were more than justified a moment later when he raised his wine glass and declared, 'A toast—to lovely ladies, exquisite cooking, *and to debts unpaid.*'

And as he said the final words his eyes promised that he had no intention of letting Seana ever forget that she now owed him—twice!

'Speaking of debts,' she said, taking immediate advantage of the situation in what she thought was a clever gambit. 'I don't suppose you'd like to tell me now just how much I owe you for the gasoline you gave me this morning?'

And when his eyes clouded ever so slightly as he recognised her motive, she pushed even further. 'Oh, come now, you wouldn't want me to feel beholden for ever. Let me see, ten gallons at . . .'

'It's not going to work, you know,' he interrupted. 'I told you I'd take a raincheck and I will. Which means you have to forget about it until the next time it rains.'

'But I couldn't do that,' she countered sweetly, all of her attention now focused on Ryan, almost oblivious to the fact they had an audience.

He met her gaze with eyes hardened with growing anger, then suddenly they cleared, the hardness replaced instantly by the mocking light she was coming to dread.

'All right,' he said very softly. 'Have it your own way; provided of course you've got a hundred bucks.'

'What?' Seana couldn't believe her ears. 'A hundred dollars? For what, may I ask?'

'For the service, of course. The gasoline wouldn't have been much use to you without somebody to bring it to you, and put it into your car, and . . .'

'Now you're being ridiculous,' she snapped.

'Maybe, but that's my price. Unless you're prepared to do what you should have done in the first place . . . and wait for a rainy day.'

Seana couldn't help but review her meagre financial situation. Did she even have a hundred dollars, she wondered, and if so, would it be worth the cost simply to make a gesture this infuriating man would probably find some way to foul up? The answer was obvious, but that didn't stop her from adding acid to her tongue when she replied.

'And I suppose you'll be asking twice that for your . . . performance in the forestry office?' she demanded. 'Or will it be three hundred, considering there was a job at stake?'

She was all too aware that Mrs Jorgensen and Ralph were now listening avidly to the exchange, but in her anger she no longer cared.

'Oh no,' Ryan replied, still with that unholy gleam in his eyes. 'The price for your job will be even higher. But don't worry about it; I'll find some . . . enjoyable way for you to work off your debt.'

'Not at my dinner table you won't,' Mrs Jorgensen interjected. 'You two can sort it out between you some other time, if you don't mind.'

And to Seana's great relief, he didn't. At least he didn't seem to; without turning a hair, he redirected the conversation on to a totally different topic, and within a minute the tension had flown from the room.

The dinner passed peaceably enough after that, although on several occasions Seana was aware of Ryan's gaze upon her. She found the conversation moving through a wide range of topics, many of them quite unfamiliar to her, but it wasn't until the two men became engrossed in a vivid argument concerning the relative merits of various breeds of truck that Mrs Jorgensen stepped in once again.

'You two can talk trucks some other time,' she said firmly, 'but not in my time. I'd rather you share a glass of port while we do the dishes, and then I'm going to fire you both out. Seana's got a long day ahead of her and I'm going to see that she gets a decent night's rest before it.'

'A proper cook should never clean up,' Ryan declared. 'So you ladies can sit with the port, and the moose and I shall do the dishes.'

Whereupon he turned on Seana with a finger raised in emphasis. 'And don't go thinking this is something special, either, young lady. If the truth were known, it's one of the rules of the house, and Mother Jorgensen knows it too.'

And that was that! Within seconds, it seemed, Seana and Mrs Jorgensen had been hustled into the living room, where they sipped at their port and listened to the truck argument resumed amidst the tinkle of plates and glassware being washed, dried and put away.

'Well,' said Mrs Jorgensen after a moment, 'you're off to a fine start with Ryan, aren't you? And the way you're going you'll have to be careful, or you'll owe him so many kisses it'll take half your life to pay off the debt.'

Seana chuckled. There wasn't much Mrs Jorgensen missed; that much was obvious. Than she realised suddenly there was an ominous silence from the kitchen, and she took just a second to think before she replied.

'Yes, it is a problem,' she replied in a deliberate stage

whisper that sounded terribly confidential but would carry, she knew, to the ears for which it was intended.

'Especially with that beard. I mean, it doesn't matter that it makes him look so *old*, but it would be . . . why, it would be like kissing an Airedale!'

'More like a wolf, and don't you forget it,' her hostess replied. 'He's not all that much older than you, although there are times, I must admit, when he seems to be older even than me.'

'And he looks it, too, with that scraggly beard,' Seana replied, still in the same carrying whisper. 'I suppose he's ugly as sin underneath it . . . or has he just got a baby face he's trying to hide?'

Mrs Jorgensen laughed aloud at that, and her laugh was followed by the sound of a piece of cutlery landing on the tiled kitchen floor.

'It's okay, Mother,' Ralph's voice boomed out. 'The geriatric just dropped a fork, that's all.

'And very good hearing he has for his age, too,' the older woman retorted. 'It's too bad he doesn't listen to what he hears . . . he might learn something.'

'Oh, I'm learning, no question about that,' said Ryan as he walked back into the living room. And although he smiled, Seana noticed that the smile didn't quite reach his eyes. Eyes that were piercing in their intensity as they probed boldly over her face, then even more boldly down the length of her body, studying, *seeing* . . . as if the caftan wasn't even there.

But what really bothered her was the way her nipples surged to erectness against the restraint of her bra, and the way her stomach fluttered and her throat began to quiver. How could any man have an effect on her . . . just by looking?

She was incapable of denying his attraction, and yet she *wanted* to deny it, wanted desperately to convince herself that Ryan Stranger just couldn't be as irresistible as her own body said he was.

And he knew it! She could tell that much just from the expression on his wide, mobile mouth, or from the calculating gleam in his pale eyes. He knew very well ... too well .. that given the slightest opportunity he could manipulate Seana as he had undoubtedly manipulated many women before her.

She was almost glad when it came time to bid both men good night; glad, and yet ...

At the very least, she thought, she'd been able to avoid an outright confrontation with Ryan. At this time in her twenty-three-year-old existence, she didn't feel quite up to meeting a challenge like Ryan Stranger head-on.

'You're going to have to watch yourself with that man,' Mrs Jorgensen quipped, hardly waiting until the door was closed on the two men before turning to Seana with a knowing smile. 'He's a heartbreaker, is Ryan, and no denying it. I just hope that you don't find yourself wishing, before the summer's out, that you'd been delegated to a different tower.'

'Oh, I'll manage,' said Seana with a conviction she didn't really feel. 'I didn't come up here to play romantic games with any man, least of all one like Ryan. In fact, that's the last thing on my schedule. I came to do a job and to see if I can't find out a bit more about myself. Despite having spent most of my life in the city, I don't really think of myself as a city person, and yet I haven't lived in the country since ... since Dad's accident, when I was twelve. So I don't really know if I'm a country person, either.'

Mrs Jorgensen was a willing and sympathetic listener, and Seana found herself telling the older woman much of what had happened to the family since her father had been so badly injured in a truck accident. Coincidentally, it had happened on the road up to White Mountain Tower, when he had lost control of his Forestry Service truck and wound up at the bottom of a deep ravine with the truck on top of him. The resultant spinal injuries had left him barely able to walk, and then only with continuing physiotherapy that was only available at the University Hospital in Edmonton.

The forest service had been a relatively small department in those days, and Sean Muldoon's knowledge and personal popularity had gained him a desk job in the city. There, despite his disabilities, he had built a strong reputation in his field until cancer stepped in to take quick advantage of his physical weakness.

But many of his interests had been passed on to his only child; Seana had grown up learning about forestry and associated fields, and found it natural as breathing to take zoology when she finally entered university.

'Except that I'm only a very smart girl on paper, Mrs Jorgensen,' she confessed. 'I've got a degree in zoology and most of my credits in forestry, but I haven't a whit of practical experience to back them up. I may get up on that tower and find that I hate it.'

Seana's mother had never been overly robust, and after her father's death had deteriorated to the point that she required considerable care. Seana had provided it willingly, but it had meant she must miss the usual summer jobs in forestry that most students used to balance their academic studies. Only after her mother's death six months before had she been able to plan a similar booster to her own studies.

'Oh, I don't imagine you'll hate it,' Mrs Jorgensen replied. 'You might be lonely, at first, but you'll have an entire little community on the radio network, and at White Mountain Tower you can be assured of your share of visitors. Me, for one.'

'And Ryan Stranger for another? Not much doubt of that, is there?' Seana replied.

'Not a whisker,' said Mrs Jorgensen. 'But don't look so concerned about it, child. Whatever else he is, Ryan's a gentleman. You wouldn't have to fear for your virtue with him unless . . .'

'Well then, I've nothing at all to fear,' Seana interjected. And when she was snuggled in her bed, eyes closed and awaiting sleep, she found herself wondering just *how* her virtue would fare on a constant diet of Ryan Stranger. What would it be like, she wondered, to be kissed by him? To feel his arms around her, his lean, powerful body against hers?

It was fine to say she hadn't come north looking for any kind of relationship, but would she really have a choice?

She drifted into sleep without finding the answer, and when morning came—only minutes later, it seemed—Seana was too busy to worry about Ryan Stranger or any other man. Right from the instant she leapt from her borrowed bed, life became a barely-controllable whirlwind of activity.

First she had to wash and dress, then sit down and eat the most enormous breakfast she had ever seen in her life—bacon, eggs, waffles with maple syrup, toast, orange juice and coffee. 'And see that you eat every bite,' said her hostess. 'It may be the last decent meal you'll get until you're properly organised up there.'

Then she had to shop for a month's supply of groceries, pick up the various Forestry Department equipment and tools she would need, then do the final bits of personal shopping that were required. It wasn't until eleven o'clock that she bade farewell to Mrs Jorgensen in the office and started the hour's drive to Spirit River for her meeting with Dick Fisher, the local Forestry man.

Dick was a small, lean man with a slightly balding

head, washed-out blue eyes and a broad grin that made her like him immediately. He was also a fountain of local knowledge, and one titbit he let slip was enough to force Seana into one last-minute shopping expedition before leaving for the tower itself.

'The joker we had up there last year was some kind of a nature freak,' Dick told her over coffee. 'He and his wife and baby ran around stark naked all summer, regardless of who was there—except for the Super, of course. Anyway, it created something of a problem because once the word got out, the old tower road just swarmed with visitors. Every weekend, right into hunting season, there'd be dozens of vehicles heading up to try and get a look at this screwball. It's one of the reasons he's not on the staff this season, and probably one of the reasons Hutton was chary about sending you up here. No telling what kind of weirdos will turn up, so be warned! Keep your door locked at night and be careful who you talk to if they show up alone or act even the least bit suspicious.'

He paused then, obviously concerned at the look of apprehension he saw on her face.

'Now don't start worrying without reason. Word gets around pretty fast up here, and it won't be long before everybody knows there's a different towerman this year.'

Again the thoughtful pause, this time followed by a brief grin and the humorous lifting of one sandy eyebrow.

'Mind you, if they find out how pretty you are, the traffic might be even worse than last year! I'd almost guarantee you'll be seeing Ralph Beatty; he's the local fish and wildlife type. And Ryan Stranger—I'll bring him up for an introduction when he turns up next— might be interesting company too. A damned good man to have around if you've any problems.'

Seana, for reasons she didn't even understand herself, didn't bother to mention that she needed no introduction to Ryan Stranger. Instead she returned to the possible problem Dick had conjured up.

'I guess I'd best stop and buy some cheap curtain material,' she replied. 'And keep a great big stick beside the bed as well, although honestly I don't anticipate any problems.'

But by the time she reached the base of the tower road, with eight miles of dirty track behind her and the worst still ahead, she wasn't quite so certain. She halted her car at the bottom of the narrow track that led up through barren poplars to the crest of White Mountain, half wishing she'd had the sense to accept Dick's offer of his four-wheel-drive forestry truck as escort.

'The road wasn't real bad when I was up there last,' he'd said. 'But I went in early and out early in the morning with the frost still in the ground. The road'll be softer now, but with the Volkswagen you shouldn't have a lot of trouble. Anyway, I'll keep my ears peeled during this evening's radio sked, so if you have any problems I can still get to you before dark.'

Seana was grateful for his concern, but her own natural stubbornness now took a hand. 'Oh, I'll be okay,' she assured him. 'I mean, even if the car can't make it, I can surely walk the last mile or so if I absolutely have to.'

Then she smiled, reneging a bit as she saw the genuine look of concern on his face. 'But please, *do* keep your ears open tonight, because I'm absolutely certain there'll be something vitally important that I'll find I've forgotten.'

Looking back now at the jam-packed rear seat of her car, she thought there couldn't possibly be *anything* she'd forgotten. The car was packed so thoroughly she couldn't even see the rear window for piles of groceries and clothing and cleaning supplies and tools. She even had a gallon jerrycan of fresh drinking water, just in case.

So why did she now feel so uncertain? When Dick had mentioned the contrariness of the gasoline generator at the tower, she had jauntily described her success at a motor mechanics course in school, and when he'd cautioned her against the rare but possible problem of a marauding black bear, she had cited with equal assurance her ability to scream loud enough so he would hear her without the radio.

But sitting alone in her car, looking at the deep ruts in the muddy road ahead of her, she wished momentarily for the assurance she had so casually expressed back in Spirit River.

'Ah well, too late now,' she muttered aloud, and slipped the car into first gear to ease it to a steady, non-skid start up the narrow track. And for the next fifteen minutes her attention was fully devoted to the problems of simply keeping the car moving, on the road, and steadily climbing despite the mud which sprayed out from the churning rear wheels.

The first mile was fairly easy, although she never got the small, overloaded car past second gear. But from that point on the road—if such was a proper description—became increasingly steeper and more twisted. Several times Seana recovered from an unexpected skid, but only when the tires contacted some long-forgotten gravel at the edge of the track.

Finally she rounded a sharpish bend to see the first spreading tops of the huge jackpines that a childhood memory told her surrounded the cabin at White Mountain Tower, and she breathed an inner sigh of relief. Too soon! There remained one truly steep grade to be climbed, and it was a grade with a vicious curve smack in the middle of it.

The car was slewing wickedly across the ruts when Seana rounded the curve, and she reached for the shift lever to jam it into first gear if necessary. Then she looked up and immediately stood on the brake pedal as an emormous shape stepped out into the road squarely in front of her.

A moose! But more astonishing—a *white* moose!

Seana gasped in surprise as the car skidded to a stop, the engine dying convulsively as her foot slipped from the clutch pedal. Then there was only silence as she and the incredible apparition stared at each other.

Seana was fascinated. And as she stared, knowing that true albinism is rare among members of the deer family, she noticed that the animal's eyes were dark, not pink.

Although there appeared no hair on the animal's body that wasn't white, the inside edges of his flickering, mule-like ears had a sooty tinge, and there was a blue-black aura to the velvet on his budding antlers. The antlers, still in the early stages of their development, had nearly a one-metre spread already, suggestive of a monstrous rack when they had grown to full size later in the year.

Seana was entranced. She just sat and stared, the arduous drive forgotten in her enthusiasm at having the opportunity to study such a rare specimen at such close range. Her eyes took in every detail, the massive withers, the pendulous, drooping muzzle and the unexpectedly slender legs that seemed almost stilt-like compared to the massiveness of the animal's body.

She felt no fear; it was far too early for the inborn rages of the rutting season that would come with the changing patterns of autumn. Instead, she felt a sense of wondrous contentment at just being able to see such a magnificent animal, wild in its natural habitat and yet so obviously unafraid.

They stared at each other for what seemed like hours, Seana almost breathless with admiration and the moose with his eyes and sensitive ears flickering constantly with the breeze as he inspected this curious invader of his domain. Finally, apparently satisfied, he turned and strode up the road, his broad, cloven hooves kicking up clots of mud as he stalked with a curious, dignified majesty up over the rise and out of sight.

It left Seana sitting alone, lost in her own thoughts even after the majestic animal had disappeared. It wasn't until nearly ten minutes had passed that she finally started up the car again and slithered precariously along the tracks of the ghostly bull moose. Five minutes later she crested the final gentle rise and slewed to a halt before the tiny clapboard cabin that snuggled beneath huge jackpines.

Home! And indeed, it seemed homely . . . just as her childhood memories recalled. A small cabin, painted in the traditional white with green trim and completely dwarfed by the height of the spreading pines and the tall steel skeleton of White Mountain Tower itself.

Home! For at least five months, perhaps as long as seven, this tiny cabin would be hers, a place in which she could recall her childhood past and look ahead to the misty outlines of the future.

Her first reaction, once she had unlocked the massive ancient padlock on the cabin door and forced it open, was one of amazement. From the outside, the small structure had promised, if not luxury, at least a degree of comfort in the isolated but picturesque location.

Inside, the promise was only that of backbreaking labour—days of it—before she would even feel comfortable sleeping there. There were mouse droppings everywhere; a packrat had constructed his unique and haphazard nest on one corner of the solid timber bunks, and the scattered remnants of the previous occupant's supplies were strewn everywhere.

Seana debated momentarily whether or not to just give it up. Right here and right now, she thought. But her stubbornness quickly took over, and almost without being consciously aware of it, she began planning the cleaning programme that she would have to begin immediately if she wanted to sleep with any degree of security that night.

'First, hot water,' she mused, stepping delicately through a jumble of mouse-gnawed packages and litter to reach the propane stove which listed unhappily against one wall. She looked it over carefully, testing each knob and connection, then strode out of the cabin and around behind, where huge propane bottles stood like metallic soldiers. Each of them was almost as large as she, and considerably heavier, but of course not one was hooked up to the regulator on the cabin wall. Worse yet, she quickly discovered by shaking them, not one had any propane anyway.

'Damn!' she muttered, then conquered her immediate twinge of alarm by looking around the rest of the site for the woodpile, reasoning that the Department could arrange to bring her fresh propane supplies in good time, and in the meantime she could manage well enough with the wood-burning airtight heater that obviously pre-dated the stove by many years.

The remains of the woodpile showed little promise, but there was enough at least to make a start, so she dragged in what wood there was and carefully laid a fire in the aged heater.

She got the tinder and kindling alight, then closed the heater's fire-door and started off in search of the spring, a metal bucket swinging from each hand.

Almost immediately, to her great delight, childhood

memories seemed to spring to life full-grown. She felt
almost as carefree as when she had walked this same
trail, with her father, as a toddling child. The spring,
however, wasn't quite as she remembered!

Sheltered in a tiny gully, it was still partially choked
with rotten ice, and the water was the colour of weak
coffee. Muskeg water, stained from the peat-like
ground through which it flowed. It would be barely
drinkable at the best of times, she realised lamely, and
worse than usual this early in the year. Still, it would
do for the washing-up, she thought, and was thankful
she'd been smart enough to bring a small supply of
drinking water.

As she knelt to fill the buckets, a saucy whisky-jack,
or Canada Jay, screamed at her from a nearby tree,
and Seana's mood immediately brightened. She knew
how easily these mischievous birds could be tamed,
dropping with their raucous, strident cries to take food
right from a person's hand, once they had learned to
trust.

Once back at the cabin, she set down the buckets so
as to force open the door, then immediately knocked
one bucket flying in her involuntary recoil from the
billowing clouds of smoke that greeted her.

With fear of a fire her most immediate thought,
Seana hesitated only an instant before charging reck-
lessly into the blinding, choking smoke to see what had
happened. There was no fire, only the billowing evidence of her own stupidity.

'I've forgotten to open the damper,' she cried aloud.
'Oh, Seana—how stupid can you get?' And she grabbed
up an old dishrag from the mouse-splattered table and
coughed her way over to where the damper handle
protruded from the blackened stovepipe.

She had to use both hands to turn it, feeling it grate
within the pipe, but at first her action only forced more

smoke into the room. Frantic now, she flung open the door of the heater to provide a draught, and was relieved to see the wood suddenly flash into fiery life as the oxygen rushed in.

'Fantastic!' she muttered, and threw in several larger sticks to help the fire along. Then she moved around, waving the rag of a tea-towel to help move the smoke and clear the interior of the cabin.

It didn't take long, but when she turned back to the stove she recoiled in alarm. The first section of stove-pipe was glowing a dull cherry red that climbed higher and higher along the pipe even as she watched.

This time her thought was first for the remaining water, and she stumbled frantically through the open doorway, her eyes streaming from the smoke and her mind barely moving. Once in the fresh air, she began to cough uncontrollably.

It took ages, it seemed, until she regained sufficient wind to follow through with her intent. And even then it took all her remaining strength to grab up the bucket, rush back inside and fling the contents into the open door of the heater.

There was a sizzling rush of steam and a booming sound that seemed to shake the cabin to its very foundations. The room filled with the scalding, blinding steam, and Seana floundered her way back to the door, terror-stricken now.

Once again a fit of coughing seized her, and she sat on the stoop with her head between her knees, oblivious to everything but the wracking pain in her throat and lungs, the queasiness of her stomach and uncontrollable lightheadedness.

The steam seemed to have taken on a life of its own, billowing inside the cabin and out of the door like a ghoulish wraith. She couldn't go in again, but she could check on her success from outside.

She ran around to the back of the cabin and stared up in even greater alarm. The pipe was *still* glowing, and now it became clear that the fire wasn't extinguished by her efforts at all; it was climbing steadily upward, and as the stovepipe grew hotter, the entire cabin was a risk.

'Oh, My God!' she cried, stumbling back to the front porch and blindly fumbling for the second bucket. She had just picked it up when something like great pincers clamped on her shoulders, and she looked up to find Ryan Stranger, eyes cold with anger, staring down at her.

CHAPTER THREE

'WHAT are you up to this time, ladybug? Still trying to live up to the nursery rhyme?' But there was no humour in either eyes or voice. Ryan was coldly, bitterly angry.

'I . . . er . . . the stovepipe,' Seana stammered. 'It's on fire . . . I don't know how . . .'

But he was no longer listening. Instead he forcibly sat her down on the stoop and turned quickly away, but not before shouting, 'Stay there!' in tones that defied argument. Then he was plunging into the cabin, stripping off his bush vest as he ran.

'Hell!' Seana jumped to her feet like a startled animal at his cry of rage, but he was already returning at full pace, sucking at two obviously burned fingers as he sprang down from the stoop and rushed to his truck.

Flinging open the vehicle, he grabbed out a tattered rug from the floor of the camper area and trotted quickly back to stand looking fixedly for an instant at the steep-pitched roof.

'Right,' he snapped, turning to fling the blanket into a small mud puddle at the edge of the cabin clearing, then treading on it until it was thoroughly soaked.

'Okay, ladybug, your turn now,' he said, 'I'm going to hoist you up on the roof and I want you to stuff this around the rain cap so you choke off all the air. All of it! Do you think you can manage that without creating another disaster?'

There was just enough mocking contempt in his voice to snap Seana out of her confusion. 'Well, of course I can,' she cried angrily—and would have said more, but he was already thrusting the sodden fabric into her hands and kneeling to give her a leg up.

'Well then, get up there and do it,' he roared, literally flinging her up on to the shingled roof. He used so much sheer strength in the manoeuvre that she hardly had to scramble at all; simply by letting the momentum carry her, she reached the crest and was able to balance easily with one foot on either side of the ridge-line as she carefully jammed the wet blanket into place.

'There! Is that good enough for you?' she demanded when no single tendril of smoke could be seen to escape. It was right; she knew that. Already the stove-pipe had lost some of its glow, although she wouldn't have wanted to touch it.

'I suppose it'll have to do,' Ryan conceded, standing with hands on hips as he stared up at her.

'Well, if you want me to change it you only have to say so,' she snapped. 'But I'd suggest you do so while I'm still up here.'

'Okay, I'll think about it,' he replied, turning away to re-enter the cabin, emerging a moment later with both buckets swinging from his fingertips. From her high vantage point, Seana was astounded to see him strolling deliberately towards the spring, paying no attention to her plight at all.

She didn't believe it at first, then believed it only too well as he disappeared out of sight in the edge of the jackpines.

'Hey!' she cried angrily. 'Damn you, Ryan Stranger, you stop right there!'

For an instant she thought he was going to just ignore her; then an indistinct shape reappeared in the trail.

'You want something?' he called back.

'Well, of course I want something. I want to come down from here!' she yelled.

'Oh, is that all?' And to her amazement he turned away again, dismissing her entirely.

'You come back!' she screamed. 'Damn you—I said come back here! You can't just walk off and leave me up here . . . you just can't!'

Only he did. Not for very long, but at least until he had filled the water buckets, which were brimming when he finally stepped into view once more. By this time Seana was almost speechless with rage, but she managed to croak out yet another demand to be helped down from the roof.

This time he merely laughed, showing her even white teeth as he looked up to where she was sitting uncomfortably astraddle the ridge.

'You sure do get cranky,' he commented, and then walked out of sight beneath the eaves. She heard—and indeed felt—the cabin door shut behind him, but he either didn't hear her cries of anger, or more likely ignored them.

It was at least five minutes before he returned to stand in the yard, looking up at her this time with quite undisguised amusement.

'Yeah, I suppose we'd better get you down from there before you fall down,' he said. 'Although personally I think that's a damned good place for you; at least you can't cause any more hassles up there. Has anybody ever told you you're something of a walking disaster area, ladybug?'

'They haven't—and I'm not,' Seana declared emphatically. 'And stop calling me that stupid name!'

'Why? It certainly fits—especially after this little performance,' he jibed. And to her amazement, he then proceeded to quote the nursery rhyme at her:

Ladybug, ladybug, fly away home,
Your house is on fire and your children will burn.

'What are you—crazy or something?' Seana raged. 'Here I am stuck on the roof and you want to quote nursery rhymes! Will you please just get me *down from here*?'

'Ah, the magic word,' he cried with apparent delight. 'Now see how easy it is to say. Please! Very simple word, but it's magic.'

'I'll give you magic!' Seana snarled—then clamped her mouth shut. Time enough to get even with this arrogant, hateful man once she had both feet safely on the ground.

'I'll just bet you will,' he replied, walking over to stand just below the eaves at their lowest point. 'Okay, come on down.'

Seana edged her way down along the steep, shingled surface, but when she reached the edge there was no ladder, no obvious means of further descent. Only Ryan Stranger standing with outstretched arms.

'But . . .'

'What's the matter? Afraid I won't catch you?' His jeering tones were a challenge that was really quite unnecessary. From this point, she realised with dismay, she could have jumped down by herself without his help in the first place. If she'd only known!

'I . . . I can manage by myself, thank you,' she cried angrily. 'If you'd just get out of the way . . .'

'No chance. Try jumping from there and you'd probably break one of those lovely legs,' he retorted. 'So for once in your life you're going to try obeying orders. Ready? One, two, three—jump!'

And she did, squarely into arms that cushioned the shock of her landing, then locked around her waist and held her firmly imprisoned as he stared down at her.

'See how easy it is. And it'll be even easier next time.'

'Next time? What are you talking about?'

He shrugged, but didn't release her. 'Just that there's bound to be a next time of some description,' he grinned. 'You're hardly safe to be left on your own.'

'That's ridiculous,' she snapped, writhing in a vain attempt to free herself as her body began to respond to the warmth of him against her. 'Will you please let me go!'

'No, I don't think so,' he replied. 'I'd just as soon hang on to you; this way I know exactly what kind of trouble you're likely to get into, if any.'

Seana raised both fists and began to pound them against the rippling muscles of his shoulders, but he only laughed and pulled her tighter against him, his eyes fixed on hers with an intensity that seemed almost mesmerising.

'I think it's about time I started collecting on some of those rainchecks,' he murmured. 'Wouldn't want to see you in debt for the rest of your life.'

'No!' The cry escaped her lips only an instant before he claimed them with his mouth. Seana struggled against him, but she might have saved her breath; he was far too strong.

She made herself rigid, determined to give him no response whatsoever, despite the quickening of her pulse and the sudden fire that spread from her middle to burn uncontrolled throughout her entire body.

Ryan ignored her lack of response for a minute . . . or was it an hour? . . . kissing her lips, then running his own lips across her cheek, down the column of her neck, back to nibble teasingly at her ear.

'You're just bound and determined to make things difficult for yourself, aren't you?' he whispered in her ear, then shifted his lips to trace lines of temptation along the line of her jaw, en route to recapture her lips.

His fingers were no longer locked behind her back; one hand held her easily while the other caressed her, stroking up and down the ridges of her spine, tracing the contours of her shoulder-blades, rubbing liquid torment into the hollow at the small of her back.

Then his lips became more demanding, teasing against her mouth, forcing a response without force, but instead with an expertise that defied Seana's experience. Despite her wish to remain unmoved, untouched, she felt her body coming alive, her breasts hard against his chest, her stomach fluttering and her legs losing their ability to hold her upright.

'My God, but you're lovely,' he whispered, his breath sifting between her lips like a warm breeze of some exotic perfume.

Her lips parted further in response to his kiss, and her arms seemed to take on a life of their own as they circled about his neck, pulling him closer to her. His beard and moustache tickled against her skin, but she felt no urge to giggle, but only to drown herself in the scent of him, the touch of his hands and body, the essence of him that was so strongly, so irresistibly male.

All Seana's willpower, all her good intentions, disappeared like the puffs of smoke from the cooling heater. All she wanted now was to get closer to him, to feel his body against hers, within her. Her fingers slid back to pluck at the buttons of his shirt, fluttering like tiny butterflies across the furry, muscled chest.

And she felt the effect it had on him, revelled in it. As his own hand slid around to open her shirt, to free her breasts to the touch of his lips, she writhed with delight, whispering his name aloud as his hands and mouth roused her to new heights, new peaks of pleasure, new and total surrender.

And then he stopped. Not gently, easily, with any consideration for the soaring lethargy of both their passions, but abruptly, cutting off their lovemaking as if with a knife.

'Sorry, ladybug, but this isn't getting your new home fit to live in,' he said cruelly, his eyes still smoky with passion as he held her away from him and deliberately caressed one breast in a gesture that cooled her own passions as if she'd been dunked in ice-water.

'We'll save this for later; right now there's work to do,' he continued, and Seana recoiled from his touch, her own eyes dark now with an anger that sprang full-grown from the coals of her surrender—her total, rejected surrender.

'You . . . bastard!' she hissed. 'You utter, contemptible bastard! Get out! Just get out of here and . . . and never come back. Never!'

'Don't be hard to get along with,' he replied easily, obviously quite unaffected by her rage. 'If you're going to make it through the summer here, ladybug, you're going to have to learn to get your priorities straight.'

'I have,' she snapped. 'And the first of them is to get rid of you!'

'Ah, you don't really mean that,' he said with a grin. 'We've already established what you *really* want. But first things first, and first is to get this stove problem sorted out. You'll likely need it for heat, if nothing else. There'll be some damned cold nights up here before summer arrives.'

'Are you deaf? I told you to get out,' she retorted hotly. 'Out. O.U.T.! I don't want you here; I don't need you here. I can fix the stove on my own, and anything else that needs fixing too!'

Ryan laughed out loud, and this time his eyes held a mockery that could only be deliberate. 'There's one thing you damned well can't fix by yourself, but we'll let that go for now,' he chuckled. 'And stop being cranky, for God's sake. I didn't want to stop any more than you did.'

Then, without warning, he grabbed her arm and dragged her over to his truck before she could think to object. 'Look at yourself,' he chided. 'Do you really want to make love looking like *that*? Not that I look much better, but this isn't supposed to be a chimney-sweeps' convention, you know.'

Seana peered into the truck mirror, then recoiled involuntarily at the face which stared back at her. She was covered in soot and her hair was all askew. Only her eyes seemed normal, peering from beneath grimy lids at a face that might almost have been made up for some dreadful comedy.

She giggled. It was impossible not to, especially with Ryan's face grinning over her shoulder. And he wasn't much less filthy than Seana herself, only in his case the soot was splashed across his forehead and cheeks in bands, as if he were an Indian preparing for war.

'See what I mean?' He laughed aloud now, and she couldn't help but laugh with him. Suddenly the thought of either of them making mad, passionate love in such a state seemed utterly ludicrous.

'I think maybe we'd best have some coffee, then we can see about making the place liveable in,' he said, and when he reached out to guide her towards the camper door, Seana followed meekly and silently. A few minutes later she was perched beside the table inside the camper, a steaming and welcome cup of coffee in her hand.

Sitting across from her, Ryan sat nursing his own coffee, staring down into the cup with a silent intensity that did nothing to provoke conversation. Seana sipped at the brew, feeling herself relax slightly as the liquid slid down to create a warm pleasantness inside her. She closed her eyes, reflecting on the good fortune that had brought Ryan to her mountain in time to keep her from disaster.

Then her eyes snapped open as reality struck. 'Just what *are* you doing here, anyway?' she asked. 'It has to be more than coincidence that you arrived so soon after I did.'

'Obviously,' he replied. 'I just thought I'd drop by and make sure they'd left you a cabin to stay in. I know these forestry jokers; it would never occur to any of them, bar Dick Fisher, of course, to make sure the shack hadn't burned to the ground or been struck by lightning or something.' Then he laughed. 'Although I suppose it wouldn't have occurred to them that you might burn it down yourself.'

Again that savage, sarcastic grin, and Seana felt her nerves tauten at the blatant chauvinism.

'Well, I hardly think it's *my* fault,' she replied hotly. 'How was I supposed to know the stupid chimney would catch fire? I don't even know *how* it caught fire.'

'Tamarack! That naked nitwit who was here last year obviously burned off all the tamarack that they cleared when they built the helicopter pad, and of course it would never have occurred to *him* to clean the chimney once in a while.'

'Tamarack? Up here?' Seana's confusion was well founded; it wasn't the type of country one would expect to find tamarack, a member of the larch family that usually grew in boggy, swampy areas.

'Yup. There was a bit of a muskeg there where the chopper pad is now, and just enough tamarack to screw up that chimney right and proper.' Ryan snorted angrily. 'Damned stuff burns beautifully, but it makes the worst soot imaginable—builds up in the chimney and then burns again if the fire gets too hot. You're damned lucky the whole roof didn't go; I hope you realise that.'

His tone was serious, and yet somehow lightly bantering as well, as if he were laughing at her from deep behind those pale eyes.

'Why'd you want to use the old heater anyway?' he asked. 'Couldn't you figure out how to get the propane stove going?'

'Of course I could. Do you think I'm completely ignorant? The reason, obviously enough, was that there isn't any propane. All the bottles are empty.'

'Oh?' He raised one eyebrow with the question. 'And I don't suppose you looked in the generator shack?'

Seana felt colour rising to her face as she remembered Dick Fisher's reminder that she'd likely find only empty propane cylinders outside the cabin, but that there should be at least two stored inside the tiny cubicle that held the generator that provided electricity for both the cabin and the tower.

She wanted to answer Ryan, but couldn't think of any reply that wouldn't make her look even sillier than she did already. He was already sliding out from behind the table, casually laying his empty coffee cup in the sink as he passed.

'I'm afraid I may have done entirely the wrong thing in Hutton's office,' he said grimly. 'You're not safe to be left alone up here, ladybug.'

And before she could reply he was out the door and holding up his hands to help her down. 'Well, let's get at it. The sooner I get things running smoothly, the sooner I can get out of your hair.'

She meekly handed over the keys to the generator shack at his request, and stood silent as he wrestled out a heavy propane bottle and connected it properly to the regulator. 'This should see you through a couple of weeks, anyway,' he said. 'Now let's go see if we can do something about that stovepipe, or it'll be cold on the mountain tonight.'

With hardly another word to Seana, he gathered up a length of heavy fencing wire that was lying about, then twisted it firmly around a small bundle of old chicken mesh from beside the woodpile. He even found the rickety old ladder and used it to climb up on the roof so he could dismantle the rain cap and then thread the wire down and into the stove below.

'Let me know when it hits bottom,' he said, and at Seana's shout he dropped easily from the roof and wrapped the free end of the wire around a short stick.

'Now comes the fun part,' he grunted. 'I'd get out of the way if I were you, ladybug. It wouldn't surprise me to have the whole shootin' match come down in a heap.'

Seana wouldn't have believed the mess he created. Tons, it seemed, of filthy soot and tar spewed down into the heater and out on to the cabin floor as he hauled the wire bundle down the length of the chimney.

And when he repeated the process, as much again came tumbling like black snow from the mouth of the heater, blackening Ryan's already dirty arms and piling up around his feet. He endured the entire performance in a silence broken only by the occasional muttered curse at the stupidity of it all, but seemed cheerful enough when he was done.

'Right, now your work can begin,' he told her. 'And I don't envy you one little bit, despite the fact that I think you deserve some consideration.'

The consideration, she discovered, was for Ryan to haul water while she scrubbed. Buckets and more buckets, until finally he announced that she would have to finish quickly because the spring was about to run out.

Then he disappeared to spend the rest of the afternoon outside, tinkering with the generator, putting away the heavy plywood shutters from the windows, even scampering like some great black squirrel up the steel skeleton of the tower to ensure that everything was in order at the top.

Seana hardly noticed his absence, she was so busy with mop and cleaning rag inside the small cabin. The filth that came from the chimney was the worst part, but mice, packrats and the former occupant had all left their indelible mark on the place.

And so, she realised, had Ryan Stranger. It was easy enough to ignore, or pretend to ignore, his presence at the tower site, but much less easy to ignore her memory of the touch of his hands on her breasts, the taste of his lips against hers.

But most disconcerting of all was the knowledge that had he not so brutally ended their lovemaking, it would have continued to the obvious result with no objection from Seana herself. Her body still tingled, her senses inflamed and aroused despite the physical effort of scrubbing at the filthy floor and walls and windows.

And what of Ryan? she wondered. Was he equally sensitive to how well they had seemed to mesh, match? Or was he immune to the aftermath of such fiery passion, able because of his obvious experience to shrug aside the feelings that must accompany such a beautiful, horrible, deliberate lovemaking?

Then suddenly he was there in the room with her. The door, flung open in a careless yet hurried gesture, crashed against the wall, sending echoes throughout the cabin.

'The radio!' he said quickly. 'Haven't you got it set up down here yet?'

She shook her head, wondering at his panic as he shot her a scathing glance and grabbed up the heavy, battery-powered forestry radio from the floor where it had been unloaded.

'Can't you do anything right?' he snapped, beckoning her attention as he moved dials and knobs until the hum of static had cleared.

'What are you talking about?' Seana retorted angrily, then glanced at her wristwatch, lying forgotten on the table where she had placed it when she started cleaning.

'Afternoon sked, obviously. Damn it, woman, you're unbelievable! Don't you understand the panic you'd cause if you didn't come in as scheduled?'

'So I forgot! Is it some kind of crime?' Seana's anger flared in direct proportion to the scorn in his eyes. 'Goodness, it must be wonderful to be a man, to always be right, to be just so perfect ... you make me sick!'

He ignored her, his ears intent on the crackling voices that issued from the radio as the afternoon schedule linked all the towers in the Grande Prairie forest in a litany of call-signs and replies.

Strangely, it brought back fond memories to Seana, pictures from her childhood that merged with the crackling sounds in a reverie she hardly realised. Until her own call-sign came in and Ryan answered it without so much as a glance in her direction.

Worse, he continued to ignore her as he recited a long list of requirements, things she would obviously be needing within the next week or so.

He was outlining the need for several more propane cylinders and half a dozen lengths of six-inch stovepipe when the absolute gall of the man struck her like a blizzard wind.

Lips thinned with anger and her face red as fire, she reached out to snatch the two-way control from his hand. Too late; even as she grabbed the microphone, Ryan had signed off, and the speed of the 'sked' had the central operator moving on to another tower.

Seanna was so angry she could almost spit, and

indeed the words she managed to force out emerged like the hissing spit of an angry cat, fuelled by her embarrassment and spurred on by her impotent rage.

'How could you do that? What possible right do you have to just . . . just take over like that? Can't you see what your little performance makes me look like? . . .'

She was still struggling for some semblance of control, still shouting almost incoherently, when his deeper voice overrode her protests.

'It makes you look quite pretty, actually,' he said, a mocking laugh firing her fury even higher. 'And if I'd left it to you, despite your good looks, young lady, you'd have missed the sked entirely, you wouldn't have known what you needed if you did make contact, and you'd probably have ended up trying to fix the radio with a hairpin or some such stupid thing. At least this way they know you're okay, and we won't have half the forestry service chasing around in the middle of the night looking for you.'

'No!' she snapped. 'I'll just have *all* the forestry service thinking . . . thinking I'm already too well taken care of, which I suppose is just what you'd like, isn't it? You're not content to come up here—uninvited, I might add—and . . . and assault me. You have to brag about it over the radio, tell the whole world!'

'Hey now, that's a bit harsh,' he replied calmly. 'I said no such thing, and you know it.'

'You implied it, and *you* know it,' she shouted even louder. 'Why didn't you just tell them all you were staying for breakfast, and be done with it?'

And to her astonishment, he grinned hugely. 'Because *then*, I hadn't been invited,' he replied. 'Now that I have . . . well . . .' The mockery was unmistakable, deliberate.

'Oh . . . go to hell!'

'Did anybody ever tell you you're a most ungrateful

brat?' he replied with maddening calm. 'Keep on acting this way and I won't stay for breakfast after all.'

Seana's reply was pre-empted by a sudden crackle from the radio, and Ryan reached out to snatch the microphone from her before she realised what was happening.

'Negative . . . negative,' he snapped. 'The only thing of any real importance is drinking water, Dick, and you can bring that up tomorrow morning on the frost, or even the day after. I've got plenty, so I'll leave the lady enough to get by on.'

The reply was so garbled by static that Seana only caught half of it, but Ryan seemed able to understand every word, a fact that did nothing to improve her temperament.

'All right, I'll stop by on my way through,' Ryan was saying in answer. 'But I don't know how late it might be; I've still got a fair bit to do here.'

The innuendo was unmistakable, and Seana splut-tered with rage as she snatched for the microphone, this time managing to get it before the sign-off.

'If he's not there in an hour—one hour—then please come up here and . . . and . . .' And what? Dared she shout over the entire network that she was already having man troubles? On her very first day? It would be enough, she realised, for the forestry superintendent to have her sacked before the season had even started.

'And what?' Ryan was looking at her, amusement lighting his eyes. Then they shifted and she followed his glance to see how he'd shifted the radio off channel. So her half-said remark hadn't been heard after all!

Flinging herself to her feet, she was already halfway out the door when Ryan replaced the dial and said, 'Sorry, Dick, I must have knocked the silly thing off the channel for a moment. Do you copy all right now?'

Seana didn't hear the reply; she was running as fast

as she could down the trail to the spring, all too aware of only the frustration tears that streamed down her sooty cheeks.

And there she stayed for nearly half an hour, hoping against hope that by the time she returned, Ryan Stranger would be gone. But it was futile, she realised. He couldn't leave without her hearing his truck, and when the time crept past without a recognisable sound, she finally stalked back towards the cabin, her mood not one whit improved.

Ryan greeted her return with a vague wave. 'Well, are you over your little tantrum?' he asked sarcastically.

'No, I'm not!' Seana retorted. 'And I'm not likely to be while you're still here. Why can't you take a hint?'

'What hint?' he retorted. 'Hints, dear child, require subtlety, which is something I fear you sadly lack— along with good manners, a sense of humour, and several other things I could name. Sometimes I really wonder why I love you at all.'

'And don't talk like that!' she snapped. 'All right; thank you for fixing my stovepipe; thank you for getting the propane stove working; thank you for getting the radio going in time for sked; thank you for . . . for everything! Now will you please go?'

'When I'm ready,' he replied softly. 'Speaking of which, it's getting on for supper time. Or am I to believe you can't cook either?'

Seana choked back an angry remark, then replied with as soft a voice as she could muster, 'Not really, no. I plan to live through the summer on instant soup.'

'*Cold* instant soup, I presume,' he replied. 'I think that might be safer, the way you've gotten on so far. Ah well, I've done just about everything else; I suppose I can cook our dinner as well.'

'You'll do no such thing!'

He looked at her, eyes half mocking, half serious.

'And tell me, dear child . . . just how do you propose to stop me? If you don't eat, you'll hardly have any strength left for another little tantrum.'

'If I didn't have to put up with you, I wouldn't need tantrums,' Seana retorted. 'You are the most infuriating person I think I've ever met!'

'Probably, but at least you can't say I'm boring,' he replied. 'Now what say you go clean up that pretty face while I get the steaks on? Or are you going to continue making a big issue of this?'

'I suppose you'll want to check that I've washed behind my ears, as well,' she muttered uncharitably, realising for the first time that Ryan had already cleaned up, presumably while she was sulking down by the spring. He had even, she noticed, changed into a fresh pair of trousers and a clean shirt.

'Don't tempt me,' he replied. 'I've left you some hot, clean water on the stove. Very hot, so be warned.'

'I'm sure I can manage,' she replied sarcastically, throwing him an angry glare over her shoulder as she walked away.

Once inside the cabin, she found herself forced to look round and appreciate just how much he had done to really help her. The floor was now relatively clean, thanks to her own efforts, but while she had been off at the spring he had not only cleaned himself up, but had unloaded her car and neatly stacked up the various supplies for her. The table was spotless and she found, to her amazement, that he had even strung a short clothes-line across one corner of the kitchen.

If only, she thought, he wasn't so . . . so damned arrogant, so totally self-sufficient and organised. And so sure of himself! He was treating her like a child and enjoying, it seemed, every minute of it. She washed her hands after ladling some cold water into the basin on the propane stove, searched out a change of clothing, then found a corner of the cabin where she wasn't visible through the windows and quickly stripped off her filthy clothes. Washing took a long time; she hadn't realised just how thoroughly the soot could penetrate through clothing. In the end she was forced to give herself an all-over sponge bath, aware every second of the time that Ryan Stranger was only a few metres away and as likely as not to walk in on her at any moment.

Or would he? she thought when the washing was done and she was safely dressed again. It was easier to conjecture about that than to allow her mind to focus on the pleasantness of displaying herself for his pleasure. She might not like him, but she couldn't deny the purely physical attraction of the man.

She returned to the camper to find it redolent with the tangy aroma of garlic and other spices as two enormous steaks sizzled in a monstrous cast-iron frying pan among heaps of thin-sliced potatoes.

Even more amazing was the bottle of red wine on the table, although the tin mugs they'd have to drink from lacked a certain flair.

'Sorry about those,' Ryan waved from his position by the stove. 'It's a bit tricky carrying good crystal around in the truck, and I didn't want to disturb you.'

'Well, thank you for that, anyway,' said Seana, and then added, sincerely, 'and really, thank you for everything you've done. I'm sorry I seemed unappreciative before, but . . .'

'But I'm insufferable, I know,' he grinned. 'Forget it and pour the wine, if you wouldn't mind. This stuff's just about done.'

To her surprise, the meal came off quite comfortably. As he had been at Mrs Jorgensen's the night before (and why did it seem like weeks ago, instead of less than a day?) Ryan proved himself an interesting and informative companion. Certainly, Seana thought, a knowledgeable one. He had an almost encyclopaedic knowledge of wildlife and their habits and a host of amusing and interesting anecdotes to relate.

She had imagined at first that she would never in a million years eat the huge meal he had prepared for her, but before she even realised it, her plate was empty and so was the wine bottle.

She looked up to find Ryan staring at her, his eyes for once neither mocking nor angry, but filled with some emotion she couldn't easily identify.

It must be the wine, she thought, or is it? He seemed friendly, gentle . . . not in the least arrogant or domineering. 'What are you staring at?' she asked, suddenly aware that the wine must have gone slightly to her head. He looked so . . . accessible, for once.

'At you; do you mind?' And his voice was as soft as his eyes. Seana felt she could drown in those eyes.

'No, I suppose not,' she heard herself reply. It was as if a stranger spoke with her voice. All her antagonism seemed to have flown away, and she was looking at Ryan for the first time without any preconceived barriers between them.

She wanted to reach out, to touch him. She could! The table between them wasn't wide; his fingers were well within reach. And then it was as if he'd read her mind; his hand moved the necessary few inches and her fingers were taken in his hand, softly as if they were terribly fragile.

'You're very lovely,' he said, the words emerging soft as butterfly wings, tantalising in their very texture. She could feel them as a tangible caress.

But his next words destroyed the effect with the sudden impact of a thunderbolt. 'I don't suppose you'd like to get out of this job now. You'll never make it through the summer, not without some kind of disaster.'

CHAPTER FOUR

SEANA pulled her fingers away as if they'd suddenly been scorched. But the inside of her, the tender, vulnerable part, was suddenly cold as ice.

'Just what do you mean by that?' she asked in a voice building with tension and warning. If Ryan meant what she thought he meant, she decided, she might very well throw something at him.

'Well, it ought to be perfectly obvious after today's fiasco,' he replied sternly, as if speaking to a wayward child. 'You're not safe to leave alone up here.'

She wanted to reply, but the words stuck in her throat. Rising abruptly to her feet, she simply stared at him, knowing her own face was chalk-white with anger, her bosom heaving as she fought for control.

'Thank you for the dinner,' she finally choked, then flung herself towards the camper doorway and leapt to the ground as if the devil himself was behind her.

The swine! she thought as she raced to the cabin, stormed inside, and then barred the door behind her. The utter swine! He'd deliberately led her on, filling her with food and wine, lulling her suspicions, and all so he could try and sweet-talk her out of staying with her job.

'I hate you!' she screamed when he hammered on the door a moment later. 'I hate you, and I never want to see you again. Go away and don't ever come back!'

'All right,' he replied, and she couldn't help but notice the weary, end-of-patience tone in his voice. 'But I'd better leave you some water before I go. Do you want to pass the buckets out here and I'll fill them from my tank?'

'You can take your damned drinking water and put it where it'll do you the most good!' she found herself screaming. 'And I hope you damned well drown, while you're at it!'

Ryan tried once more to convince her, but she ignored his voice and devoted her energies to blowing up the air mattress she'd brought for the narrow wooden bunk in the cabin. To hell with him! she thought, and was glad when he finally retreated with a muttered oath she didn't quite catch.

A moment later she heard his truck start up, and watched from the corner of her vision as he swung the vehicle around and headed off down the narrow track, his headlights playing like moonbeams ahead of him as he went.

'And good riddance, too!' she shouted, knowing he couldn't hear. But somehow it made her feel better, although it was much, much later, when she finally got to sleep, and all she could think about in her restlessness was Ryan Stranger and his deceitful ways.

She was in a better temper when the whisky-jacks woke her in the morning, followed a moment later by the arrival of Dick Fisher with several huge plastic rubbish bins filled with pure, clean town water. He didn't stay, pleading the need to get down again before the road softened too much, and Seana was in some ways grateful for that.

Her temper might have improved, but far more important was her determination to prove Ryan Stranger wrong. How dared he so blithely assume her incompetent on the basis of a single incident? Well, she'd show him, if it took her all summer to do it!

And as the spring days passed, with early summer making its presence felt more each morning, Seana gradually fell into a solid working routine, focussing all her attention on the job at hand. She checked temperatures and rainfall, followed the constant chatter of static-distorted voices on the radio and made herself totally conversant with the country for which she was responsible.

She spent most of each day in the tower cupola, using her powerful binoculars to pick out every salient detail of the rough timber country that spread in every direction.

And she made friends! She swapped recipes with Marie Duval at Bald Mountain Tower, far to the south, and tried—by radio and with questionable success—to teach the art of bread-making to Mike Rosichuk, her nearest tower neighbour. Mike was an ageing bachelor whose one great ambition in life was to learn to make proper bread, but he seemed doomed to failure, always running out of something or facing some real or imagined emergency that interfered with his baking.

In return for the lessons, however, he passed on a host of knowledge, gained through years of hunting, trapping and fire-watching in the Burnt Hills and the Grande Prairie forest.

It was Mike's position on Saddle Hills tower that Seana combined with most often to check the exact position of any smoke sightings, taking cross-references and plotting the locations on the large forestry maps in the tower.

And it was Mike's extensive knowledge that helped her through her first few sightings, all of which involved not forest fires, but those caused by farmers clearing land and burning their stubble and trash on the fringe landholdings to the north of the Burnt Hills. By law, the farmers were required to apply for burning permits, which allowed all forestry personnel to control not only the time of burning, but to know which fires were of known origin and control and which must be monitored for possible danger. In practice, however, too many farmers ignored the requirement, so that towermen and rangers ran a constant temperature in their attempts to keep up with the dozens of smoke sightings that occurred each morning during the spring burning season.

It was easier for Seana because of Mike, whose knowledge helped him to pinpoint each man-made fire with uncanny accuracy and lead the rangers to the exact quarter-section being burned off.

Seana quickly lost her initial trepidation about climbing the seemingly flimsy tower, which was capped by a small cupola that provided a three hundred and sixty-degree view of the surrounding landscape. By the end of the first week she was scampering up and down like an agile squirrel.

The tower was a naturalist's paradise, and Seana often found her attention diverted by the native wild-life that frequented the region. She took to climbing up each morning well before dawn, giving herself a bird's eye view of the morning panorama. She saw white-tailed and mule deer on occasion, and less frequently the mighty elk, massive antlers still swathed in velvet. There were moose in plenty, although she never saw the white one and began to wonder if she had really seen him at all. Could it, she wondered, have been some ghostly hallucination?

In the evenings, once the ever-later dusk had gathered in soft shadows around her cabin, she would sit and watch as the silent great horned owls pursued their prey among the night creatures which sought food near the cabin.

The lack of human companionship was far less of a problem than she had anticipated. Because of the radio network she felt almost as if she were part of a family, and it was impossible to be lonely with the radio serving as a sort of umbilical cord linking her to so many faceless voices, each with an individual personality.

Her imagination put a gnome-like face to Mike Rosichuk and the various other tower people, but it couldn't, for some reason, dismiss the one face she decided she would rather forget entirely. At least, she thought, Ryan seemed to have taken her message to heart; she neither saw nor heard from him, although his name was often enough on the radio as he seemed to visit every tower but her own.

The occasional rains had thoroughly softened up the road to her tower, making it impassable unless there was extremely good reason for its use. This, too, contributed to the lack of visitors, as the forestry people knew better than to tear up a road without good reason.

But the road was relatively dry by the time Seana's supply of drinking water was nearly gone, and since nobody seemed to have time to bring any, she asked on the Friday evening sked if she might chance driving out to Spirit River the next morning to get fresh water and some other, less vital supplies.

The answer was unexpected; she wasn't to leave the tower because she'd be getting fresh water delivered that very night, and she should expect visitors on the following day as well. Interference, however, prevented her from getting any more details, and she sat through her dinner wondering about it.

Wondering . . . and suddenly as excited as a child at Christmas. Her first visitors; discounting of course the intrusion of Ryan Stranger. But who could it be?

'Strange,' she said aloud. 'A month ago it would have worried me terribly, but now I don't care who it is that's coming. I guess I haven't adapted as well as I thought.'

Then she laughed, idly wondering if talking to herself aloud might be a sign of something more than poor adaptation to the relative isolation.

And when no vehicle arrived by nine o'clock, she began to really worry, especially as she had postponed her evening bath to avoid being caught in the tub.

But that, too, gradually became irrelevant, and she sat calmly on the porch sipping tea made with the last of her good water, simply waiting patiently. The radio said somebody would come ... so they would. She had faith in the radio.

The first muted rumblings of a truck engine filtered gently through the night stillness, sounding at first like the distant growl of some huge animal. Seana listened, growing increasingly impatient as the first beam of headlights flicked across the tops of her jackpines, then disappeared as the truck moved down into the last gully. Finally she saw the lights again, and a moment later it rumbled into the clearing, blinding her as it moved forward to park squarely in front of the cabin.

'Well, well, ladybug ... don't you look all peaceful and quiet in the moonlight!'

Ryan Stranger! Seana felt her face go suddenly hot, and the hackles at the back of her neck stiffened in recognition of that hateful, haughty voice. She answered his greeting, but the hostility in her voice was ill-disguised.

'Good evening, *Mr* Stranger. And to what do I owe the questionable pleasure of this unexpected visit?'

'Just playing water-boy. Dick's truck broke down this afternoon, so we did a bit of a switch. Hope you don't mind too much.'

'Not at all,' she replied. But she did! Why did it have to be him, of all people?

He didn't reply, but immediately busied himself heaving down the plastic containers of clean, cold fresh water and stacking them one by one on the porch of the cabin. Seana could only watch, unable to help because of the weights involved, but knowing she should at least be preparing fresh tea or coffee to offer him when he was done.

And instinctively, she knew that despite her muddled and ambivalent feelings towards Ryan, she couldn't in conscience avoid the obligations of traditional bush hospitality. So she withdrew into the cabin and got the coffee pot, returning to the porch only long enough to dip it into one of the new water containers. She didn't bother to light her pressure lamp, but instead lit two of the candles she'd come to use instead. Then she sat down and waited, gazing at the gentle dance of the flames, and the shadows that played within the open grate of the heater that radiated a comfortable glow into the cabin.

Only when the coffee was ready did she step outside to call Ryan, but she didn't get the words out before his upraised finger, ominous in the silver moonlight, bade her to silence. And as she tiptoed over to where he sat in silence near the corner of the porch, she saw the reason.

It was the white moose, gleaming like a ghost in the soft light as he stalked silently up the roadway, the bell beneath his chin swinging gently and his now-enormous antlers, still covered in velvet, carried like weightless shadows atop the mule-like head.

In the uncertain light he moved like a vision in a sort of slow-motion movie, his long, fragile-looking legs taking short, almost dainty steps as he moved closer and closer to the cabin. Despite the night stillness, he seemed more quiet still, moving like a wraith, a ghost from some ancient Indian legend. Seana, who had seated herself near Ryan when first viewing the animal, felt herself shifting even closer as the huge shape drifted in and out of the shadows, moving always nearer to the parked vehicles.

The seconds passed like hours, but suddenly Seana felt Ryan's arm close round her waist, gently, as if she, too, were something fragile in the moonlight. And neither of them seemed to breathe as the ghostly bull moose stepped nearer, huge nostrils fluttering at the scents in the night wind. And it seemed as if in that moment her own senses became somehow sharper, and she could see the dark eyelashes against the moose's shining dark eyes and white hide, could smell the pungent odour of the coffee within the cabin, the fresh, clean scent of the water in the barrels nearby and the warm, husky smell of the man so close to her, so close and yet somehow far, far away, lost in his own enchantment at the ghostly vision before them.

Her eyes dropped from the moose to pick out the curling, shadowy tendrils of Ryan's hair and the strong, clean-lined planes of his face above the flame of his beard where the moonlight struck it.

The hand at her waist hadn't moved since he had placed it there, but she was conscious still of it as a negligible weight against her hip. His fingers didn't move, but there was a curious sensuousness to the imperceptible touch and she had to resist the urge to shift even closer to him, to draw some of the vibrant male strength she could feel.

He seemed not to move, not even to breathe, and Seana realised in that instant that she, too, was breathing only in light, shallow draughts, her own body knit into a rigidity that belied her physical awareness of the man and her spiritual awareness of the huge forest giant before her.

Far in the distance, muted by the thickness of the jackpines and the barriers of hill and valley between, the moon-song of a coyote filtered through as a haunting, distant melody, and then another joined in and the song swelled . . . and yet another, and another . . . and it became a symphony of music from another place, another time, another world. Because Seana and Ryan Stranger stayed unmoving and the ghostly, shimmering bull moose seemed not even to hear.

A hunting owl, silent as a wraith on powder-feathered wings, stooped for a careless mouse in the chopper-pad clearing, but again the moose seemed indifferent, though his long, mule-like ears seemed to twitch slightly at the animal's tiny squeak of dying.

The bull reached the edge of Ryan's truck and dipped his muzzle to sniff at the vehicle's bumper, the huge antlers carefully kept from touching the metal-clad body of the camper and the splayed but somehow dainty hooves pawing only slightly at the ground below. The animal's snuffling investigation became audible then, and with the sound he lost some of his phantom veneer. Seana felt it, and so did Ryan, who for the first time tightened his grasp on her waist so that she became aware of his touch as a distinct, physical thing.

The moose walked entirely round the vehicle, each long-legged, cautious pace seemingly in slow motion. The closeness and the effects of the moonlight on its snowy coat made it seem larger than it really was, though Seana knew the animal would stand more than two metres at the shoulder, with most of its height in the disproportionately long legs. The massive antlers, still covered in the velvet in which they had grown, looked as if they were covered in heavy frost that was only just beginning to feel the touch of summer's heat. And near the tips of the antlers, the velvet was beginning to shrink and peel; within another few weeks the moose would be spending all his spare time working the antlers against small trees and bushes to relieve him of the itchy, peeling velvet.

Having thoroughly inspected Ryan's truck, the moose paused briefly, then strode purposefully forward to give the same attention to Seana's tiny car, which was truly dwarfed by the size of the visitor.

And only then did it seem to notice the cabin and the statue figures on the porch. Dipping its head, the massive antlers swaying like some grotesque clown's hat, the moose stepped one single space forward, and Seana felt herself tauten inside with the first hint of fear. Then she became even more strongly aware of Ryan's hand at her waist, pressing her over against his shoulder as if bidding her not to move, not to even breathe.

Another step, head even lower, and Seana could feel the man beside her tensing as the animal's enormous ears wriggled like separate beings as it tested the night air for information about what its weak eyes were seeing.

A third step, and she could see the large, sensitive nostrils quivering and the baleful eyes, now somehow red in the moonlight, peering directly at them. The animal's ghostliness had changed with its nearness; now it was malevolent, a powerful, vivid and dangerous strength that overshadowed the human presence on the mountain.

Seana cuddled closer to Ryan, no longer needing any urging but feeling as if she could somehow draw from his calmness and his own solid, elemental strength.

Then, so quietly she could hardly believe it, the moose started backing away, moving a dozen quick steps to the rear and then turning for a final look at the cabin and its human figures before turning to stalk off as silently as it had come.

When the animal reached the shadows at the edge of the tower clearing, it was as if it vanished in thin air, leaving Seana with her waist locked in Ryan's strong right arm and her eyes straining to follow the ghost as the familiar night sounds returned to the clearing.

Neither she nor Ryan spoke, but she could feel the tension going out of him, to be replaced with a surge of physical awareness that seemed to tingle through his fingertips to rouse her own sensuality. She suddenly became aware that her left hand, though she couldn't remember putting it there, was across his broad shoulders, her fingers tangled in the shock of curls at his nape. And she could tell also that he was acutely aware of her touch, and of the curves of her body against him.

His fingers were moving, tracing gentle, tantalising designs on the miraculously sensitive curve of her hip. She felt in one part of her mind that she should move away, but her body was still mesmerised, both by Ryan's touch and by the splendid primitiveness of what they had just seen. If anything, she moved closer, feeling her breasts tauten as his touch moved into the small of her back, moving in small, delicious circles of pleasure.

She turned her head towards him, knowing his eyes would be on her, his lips ready to claim her own. The place, the moment, held magic that would hold them both, and if he kissed her she would erupt like tinder-dry forest to the torch, without even a show of resistance.

The thought sobered her, but not enough. Green eyes, glowing with an unholy light in the glitter of the moon, locked with her own and she saw the gleam of teeth flashing against the burnished glow of his beard, felt the total, animal awareness of her as a woman.

His lips moved towards hers, but when they touched it was only briefly, tenderly, the kiss one might bestow upon a baby. And in his eyes she saw the knowledge that he *could* have taken her, and that he knew how easy it would have been—perhaps even better than she.

Seana stiffened, and as if he read her thoughts Ryan dropped his hand from her waist. She moved even more quickly, pulling her hand away from his neck and springing to her feet, almost running as she shouldered open the cabin door and made her way to the table. She was shaking uncontrollably, her face and neck were on fire, but most obvious was the curious weakness in her legs and the prickly, over-sensitive heat where his fingers had rested on her hip.

She was astounded to find that the coffee was still hot, steam rising from the cups and from the pot on the stove. It seemed like hours they had been on the porch, yet it must have been only moments.

She turned to the doorway as Ryan entered, moving in a long, catlike stride to stand looking down at her where she stood with a cup in each hand. His eyes were alive; she could once again feel his desire for her, his purely physical need of her body, her very soul.

She fended it off by handing him one of the cups, which he took with a silent nod and the mocking lift of one shaggy eyebrow. He didn't sit down, but stood there cradling the cup in two hands, sipping slowly at it and then drinking the remainder in one long, slow draught. Then he handed it back.

Seana wanted, inconceivably, to rush into his arms, to feel them closing around her, to bring back the magic of a few minutes ago, and to make new magic. But she also feared her own reactions, knew somehow it wasn't the time, perhaps not even the place. And obviously Ryan felt it too.

He bent to kiss her, again that chaste, friendly, tender kiss, without fire, without any feeling of riotous emotion. Then he stepped away, without touching her in any way except so fleetingly with his lips.

'It's late; you'll be needing your sleep,' he whispered—and was gone, as silently and ghostlike as the giant white moose. Seana stood unmoving as his truck grumbled to life and swung round to head off down the road. She wanted to wave, to make some gesture, but the feeling of rejection was too strong, too disappointing.

She was in her bed and nearly asleep when she realised she hadn't even asked him about her visitor the next day. He would have known, surely—or would he? She touched at the brand-like spot on her hip and thought that Ryan Stranger knew altogether too much, where she was concerned. Certainly, in retrospect, he knew better than she; he had saved the magic.

The morning dawned cold and misty, a direct contrast to the evening before and a circumstance that would have delighted Seana had she been awake to see it, since it would mean minimal tower duties and more time for her as yet unknown visitor. But she wasn't awake when the whisky-jacks began their morning scolding; she didn't even hear the growl of the car as it worked its way up the steep track. Her first waking realisation was of a loud thumping on the cabin door, making her leap from the bunk and grab for her clothing with almost comic haste.

Then she flung open the door and exclaimed with delight at the sight of Mrs Jorgensen, laden with parcels and scowling in mock fierceness.

'What have you been doing with yourself up here—staying up all night with the coyotes?' the grey-haired woman demanded. 'Or might wolf be a better term? I was surprised not to find Ryan's truck parked here when I arrived this morning.'

'Lord, are there no secrets in this world?' Seana asked, covering her embarrassment with jest. 'I thought I came up here for privacy!'

'All things are relative,' Mrs Jorgensen smiled. 'Now how about getting the coffee on . . . I could do with a cup or two, and I know Ralph will drink half a dozen. He'll be here in half an hour or so, I imagine, so you'd best get it on and keep it hot.'

While Seana busied herself getting the coffee together, Mrs Jorgensen began opening the parcels to reveal fresh, still-warm bread and breakfast rolls and succulent Danish pastries. 'You can't have all this,' she cautioned Seana. 'If we don't leave some for Ralph he'll start in on your grocery supply, and you'd end up facing starvation before the next grub run if he did that!'

Seana laughed, then sobered suddenly with the realisation that she had virtually nothing substantial to feed herself that day, let alone visitors. She had long since disposed of her fresh meat supplies, and having discovered a personal aversion to the noise of the generator, she had since turned the fridge into a storage cabinet and was living exclusively from tins.

'Goodness, don't worry about that,' Mrs Jorgensen laughed when Seana confessed her concern. 'I just *happen* to know that Ralph netted a poacher yesterday, and if he doesn't show up with some prime venison or moose steaks I'd be very surprised. Of course he's *supposed* to dispose of the meat to local Indians or welfare cases, but he'd be a strange fish-and-wildlife officer if he didn't think of a pretty girl like you being a needy recipient. Not that we'd ever mention such a thing, mind you. The powers of the system aren't to be trifled with, not at all.'

And as she had predicted, Ralph arrived with an enormous moose tenderloin, though he declared it was beef and wouldn't be shaken in his statement.

'It should do the two of you for dinner,' he declared,

and laughed when Seana insisted it would keep her in meat for a week at least.

'Not if you agree to the rest of my proposal,' he said. 'There's a dance on tonight at Spirit River and I've already conned Hutton into letting you spring free . . . if you'd like to come, of course.'

'I'd love it,' Seana declared without the slightest hesitation. The chance to be among people—*crowds* of people—again seemed like a breath of spring.

'Great! There's no real fire threat, but it could be the last chance you'll have to take a day off if the weather dries off, and I think it will.'

He tossed down the remainder of his coffee. 'I've got to make a patrol over to the B.C. border, so it might be seven o'clock by the time I get back. If I'm early I'll join you for dinner, but don't depend on that.'

'No dinner, no dance,' Mrs Jorgensen declared firmly. 'I know how the booze flows at these country dances, my lad, and while you mustn't take this personally, I don't think much of you going anywhere near that place on an empty stomach, not with the roads as they are.'

'Yes, Mother,' he replied dutifully, but didn't bother to try and hide the amusement in his eyes.

It wasn't until he'd gone that Seana realised she had nothing . . . absolutely nothing . . . that was suitable for any such occasion. But again Mrs Jorgensen came to the rescue.

'It isn't that I'm psychic, but I had a feeling this would happen when Ralph phoned the boss,' she said. 'So I brought along the caftan *and* your shoes and even a handbag that should go with it,' she laughed. 'And you'll probably start crying the blues now that Ralph's already seen you in that dress, but too bad.'

It wasn't Ralph's reaction Seana had been thinking of, but she wisely said nothing. Indeed, why should she even imagine Ryan might be attending the dance? He'd not mentioned it to her. Then she sobered; what right did she have to think he would mention it . . . if he were taking somebody else? She quickly thrust those thoughts aside and began planning for the arduous process of washing her hair and having a proper bath in the small plastic wading pool she had bought specially for that purpose.

Mrs Jorgensen took over the cooking duties that evening, declaring that there was a trick to dealing with fresh moose meat that Seana could only learn by watching. She sliced the tenderloin into thick two-inch slabs, then heated Seana's heavy cast-iron frying pan until it was smoking. When the coarse-grained meat hit the hot iron, that was a flash of searing, sizzling smoke, and almost before it had settled Mrs Jorgensen was turning over the slabs of meat to sear the other side as well.

Then she removed the whole thing from the stove and allowed the pan to cool somewhere before continuing to cook the steaks slowly. Ralph arrived just as they were done, and put his seal of approval on the process by eating three enormous slices with fresh rolls and salad.

Seana was surprised at the delicate flavour of the coarse-textured meat, and the fact that once through the crusty, flavourful exterior, the meat was just cooked to that perfect state where rawness gives way to pink, tender succulence. She ate one small steak, then greedily devoured another, astounded at her own appetite.

The two women quickly cleared away the dishes, then Ralph was sent out to smoke on the porch while Seana changed into the caftan and finished her preparations for the evening. His approval was obvious when the transformation was complete.

'My, my . . . I'll have to carry around a big stick tonight just to beat off the competition!' he commented, and Seana was pleased that he didn't mention having seen the dress before. On his way back from patrol he had changed into a soft grey suit and looked quite terrific himself, she thought.

They escorted Mrs Jorgensen down the mountain and on to the paved highway leading to Spirit River, but when they turned in at Spirit River, she waved gaily and carried on towards home. A few moments later and they joined the ranks of vehicles, most of them pick-up trucks, outside the local community hall.

The hall, inside, was a kaleidoscope of moving, shimmering colour, with dancers in everything from blue jeans to ballgowns whirling to music so loud it was deafening. Within an hour, Seana felt as if she had been dancing all night, having hardly had a break since their arrival.

But now the pace was slowing, with only the more exuberant dancers whirling to the strains of a square-dance Seana knew she could never follow. Ralph had slipped away to—as he put it—consult with some of his acquaintances, and Seana was gathered immediately into a chattering clutch of women whose partners also had stepped out for some liquid refreshment.

There were no strangers in the group. Through the magic osmosis of the so-called moccasin telegraph, it seemed that everyone in the hall knew who she was, why she was there, and what role she played in the far-flung rural community. Several of the women claimed to have known her father; one or two even asserted to having seen Seana as a child, but they were united in assuring she could not feel left out. She had, indeed, already danced with several of the district's young men and was pantingly grateful for the chance to rest.

One of the women was busy relating a long-winded tale about something to do with moose when Seana's attention was suddenly diverted by a splash of colour near the door. From that instant she ceased listening, her every sense centred instead on the familiar copper brightness of hair and beard. Then the face of Ryan Stranger swam into focus, his teeth bared in a happy grin.

But the grin was not for Seana; it was for the tall, shapely girl whose blonde tresses streamed out behind her as Ryan immediately swung her into step with the music.

Where Ralph had gone to considerable trouble to dress for the occasion, Ryan—like many of the other men in the room—had equally obviously come straight to the dance from the bush. He was wearing the same faded shirt and scarlet vest as when Seana had first met him, and his sun-faded jeans hung down over fancy fringed and beaded moccasins.

And yet he didn't look scruffy or unkempt; merely primitive, alive with a vibrant, vivid life-force. He seemed to loom above all the other men in the place, including Ralph who was at least three inches taller. His dancing, she noticed, was exquisite; he moved on the dance floor as he did everywhere else, with the grace and smoothness of a huge cat.

He didn't see her. She made doubly certain of it by turning her back to the floor and pretending interest in the conversation around her. But a few minutes later Ralph returned and immediately swung her out into a change of tempo that had them waltzing slowly to music that was much more in keeping with the way they were dressed.

She allowed him to hold her a touch too close for comfort, unwilling to recognise the stubborn desire for Ryan to see them together, to notice her, to somehow be affected by the knowledge that she was attending the dance with somebody else. As he was!

She glanced past Ralph's massive shoulder, not even bothering, now, to try and convince herself that she wasn't deliberately seeking out Ryan Stranger and his lovely companion. And suddenly her eyes were captured by mocking green orbs that seemed to leap at her with animal vividness from only inches away. She saw one copper eyebrow raise slightly as Ryan nodded a greeting, but the bulk of her attention was caught by the girl with him, wrapped as close to Ryan as his shirt.

Seana nodded a greeting of her own, then deliberately turned back to snuggle into the hollow of Ralph's shoulder, angry that she should be so affected by the encounter. As they spun a moment later, she felt Ralph nod his own greeting to his friend, and wondered what, if anything, he would say when the number had ended.

She was slightly miffed, therefore, when the red-haired bushman didn't stop to visit with them during the ensuing interlude. He disappeared outside with his blonde companion almost before the music ended, and hadn't returned when the band finished its rest.

But if he was absent in person, he was all too obviously present in spirit, Seana found. It seemed his name was on the lips of almost every woman she spoke to during the break, and while several seemed intent on linking it with that of his blonde companion, several others found ways to associate Ryan with Seana herself!

Seana had thought herself quite well reconciled to the fact that few secrets existed in a community where radio played such an important role, but she was stunned by the degree of knowledge displayed about her own situation and Ryan's involvement in it.

One woman, with even less subtlety than most, did her level best to prise still more information from Seana, while several others attempted to make far more than was warranted out of the fact that he hadn't yet asked her to dance.

Suddenly the evening took on a chilly aura, something alien and uncomfortable. Seana felt as if she was some sort of freak, displayed for the entertainment and amusement of the locals. And she didn't like it, not at all.

Worse, there was no escape. The evening, for these hard-working, hard-playing rural folk, was just beginning, and for Seana to leave too early, even pleading the time-honoured excuse of a headache, would only lead to even worse speculation. That, she decided, was something she could very definitely do without.

So she danced with Ralph and the host of other young men who flocked around her like bees to honey, throwing herself into the dancing, forcing herself to exude the carefree spirit of the evening. Until the next bracket of slow waltzes, when she heard a familiar voice over her shoulder, and a familiar hand took her wrist to spin her close against Ryan's chest, her head tucked beneath the flaming bush of his beard.

CHAPTER FIVE

'You seem to be enjoying yourself,' he muttered as she vainly fought against the mighty pressure of his arms. Seana didn't reply; she was too busy trying to stifle the thundering of her heart as it threatened to burst from her at the unexpected proximity of Ryan's body.

It was frightening. Here she'd been dancing all evening with a host of attractive and attentive young men, but only this one had the power to turn her knees to rubber, to make her pulse race with fearful awareness of him.

He didn't even appear to notice her struggles, but spun her through the tide of dancers with never a false step, never a hint that he knew—and he did!—how much his fingers at her spine were affecting her.

His every touch was a caress, a practised, deliberate effort to rouse her body to needing him, wanting him. And Seana did her absolute best to keep her reactions secret. She deliberately thought of Ralph, of a boy she had known at school, another at university. All to no avail. Before the first waltz was over she was attuned to Ryan's dancing style, moulded to him and flowing with him across the floor as if they were alone in the room.

He flatly, almost rudely, rebuked an attempt by one man to cut in as the second number began, and this time he kept Seana slightly removed from him, where he could look into her eyes as he talked.

'You didn't tell me you were coming here tonight.' It was almost an accusation, but not quite. And how to answer? She could be frankly honest, or . . .

'You didn't ask.' And there was no expression in her voice; she made certain of that.

'I wouldn't have thought you could get away.'

She laughed, cruelly and quite deliberately. 'There are ways of arranging these things.'

'Provided, I assume, that the incentive is strong enough.' And that definitely wasn't a question; the look in his eyes assured Seana of that much. His eyes were hard, flat, not angry but nonetheless chilling in their intensity.

'Frankly, I can't see what difference it makes,' she replied as lightly as she could.

'Obviously.' Then his eyes embarked on a minute inspection of her face, her hair, her throat. But still they remained hard, unwelcoming.

'Look, if it upsets you, there's no law says you have to dance with me,' Seana snapped, letting her own emotions slide just a trifle but not really caring.

'I make my own laws,' he replied with a grin that wasn't even remotely reassuring.

'So I've heard,' she retorted, 'although I didn't realise any of them involved turning a simple duty dance into some kind of interrogation.'

'Duty dance? Is that what you think?'

'Isn't it?' She kept her voice light, but her eyes were now as alive with emotion as his had ever been. Only it was anger, frustration at being unable to enjoy dancing with him as she had during the first number.

'Hardly. I've been wanting to dance with you ever since I realised you were here tonight,' he replied.

'So I noticed,' Seana replied drily, her eyes shifting to where Ryan's blonde partner was plastered up against Ralph, who didn't seem to mind a bit.

'Jealousy doesn't become you, lady-bug.' There was mockery in the voice, but something else, also.

Seana made her voice as cold as she could. 'Jealousy

wouldn't even *occur* to me,' she replied. 'At least not where you're concerned. Or do you think I'm jealous of Ralph's attention to your . . . friend?'

He laughed, laughter like brittle spring ice. 'Try lover, it's a bit more accurate,' he said. 'Are you?'

'Am I what?' She had to ask that question; Ryan's previous statement had struck like a stiletto at her heart, especially after hearing comparable comments from some of the local women about his relationship with the blonde.

'Jealous of Ralph,' he chided. 'What's the matter . . . aren't you listening?'

Seana sighed. 'Not really, I suppose,' she replied. 'I don't really think any of this is important.'

His chuckle was ominous, almost threatening. 'I suppose all the barnyard hens have been cackling about me again,' he said.

Seana pulled back farther away from him, giving free rein to her growing anger and hurt. 'If they have, it could only be about your extraordinary conceit,' she snapped. 'Do you mind if we stop this now? I've had about all I can take.'

He smirked down at her, then raised his eyes and Seana followed his gaze to realise they were now on the edge of the throng closest to where the gaggle of local women was gathered.

'Not quite all,' he said—and grinned savagely before pulling her close to him, his mouth closing on hers with a deliberateness Seana couldn't resist. It was a brutal, demanding kiss, taking all and giving nothing. And yet it had the desired effect; despite her anger, she felt her body begin to respond to him, and he felt it too.

He crushed her closer, continuing the kiss beyond all logic, beyond her ability to breathe, to think. And when he finally released her, he made it brutally clear that the entire exercise had been tailored to his own peculiar logic.

'There! That'll give them something to really gossip about,' he sneered. And before Seana could react, could . . . hit him, kick him, fly into a screaming rage, whatever . . . he was gone. She was left standing there with her mouth open, stunned with the assault, the abruptness of his departure, but mostly by the knowledge that he was right. The women would talk. And she could only imagine too well what they'd be saying.

Ralph, fortunately, didn't talk about Seana's unnerving confrontation with Ryan. He'd seen it; she knew that. But gentle Ralph would never add to her pain by even mentioning it, and she was glad of his silent consideration during the long ride home to her cabin.

Equally pleasant was his reluctance to seek an invitation to stay . . . for whatever reasons. He merely kissed her lightly on the brow at the cabin door, voiced his goodnight, and was gone without the slightest bit of hassle.

If only her inner turmoil could be so easily dismissed, she thought as she lay sleepless long after he had driven back down the mountain. But Ryan Stranger had fixed that, and she knew she hadn't heard the last of the red-bearded bushman's deliberate lovemaking. With luck it would be only a nine-day wonder, but the isolated life-styles of most district residents could as easily make a full meal out of that single mouthful of deliberately-contrived gossip.

Seana tried counting sheep in a bid to get to sleep. Then she tried rabbits, deer and even moose. Nothing seemed to work. Her mind kept drawing up images of statuesque blondes and mocking, knowing green eyes, no matter what else she tried to think of. It was nearly dawn before she finally slept.

It was marginally easier in the morning, which arrived far too early for Seana's tired body. And it grew easier with each passing day, then, although the first couple were fraught with wisecracks over the forestry radio network and she was forced to reply with a lightness she couldn't feel.

Of equal concern was the growing spate of warm weather, combined with the onset of school holidays. As the bush grew steadily dryer, making it uncomfortable even in the pine-shaded cabin, Seana came to hate the holidays with a passion previously reserved for warm, sunny Sundays and thoughts of Ryan Stranger.

It seemed that each day was hotter than the one before, and each day also brought a new crop of visitors to White Mountain. Her daily routine became a treadmill of rising at dawn to perform her personal chores, then spending virtually the entire day explaining to people that no, they couldn't climb the tower for a look around, and no, their children couldn't climb it either, and no, her cabin wasn't open for inspection ... it was her home; and supposedly private. She eventually took to spending the entire day in the cupola atop the tower, having made a point of locking both cabin and car before taking her binoculars, books and radio equipment with her to the relative security above.

It meant a great deal of shouting down to visitors who *all* seemed incapable of understanding why they couldn't be allowed to join her, and often she found herself becoming violently angry as they swarmed round the cabin, peering into windows and scattering gum and candy-bar wrappings everywhere. But it did seem marginally better than having to confront them at ground level.

As July passed into August without let-up in the severe drought conditions, Foresty authorities attempting to restrict access to the forests had their hands full. It was worse for Seana, because she was almost surrounded by relatively settled country. People didn't look at the Saddle Hills as actual *forest*. There wasn't much evergreen timber among the welter of poplar and birch regrowth, and the convenience to Grande Prairie made the tower a favoured picnic spot for many weekend visitors.

With virtually all her acquaintances directly or indirectly associated with the Forestry Department, Seana got few really welcome visitors. Everybody she knew was too busy working for socialising as small fires cropped up almost daily somewhere in the region.

Ralph Beatty managed to stop by on the occasional Sunday evening, and between him and her forestry radio, Seana could keep a reasonable up-date on events in the district, but Ralph—either by accident or design—never mentioned Ryan Stranger, and Ryan himself never came near White Mountain Tower.

The most difficult aspect of Ralph's visits was her growing concern that he was becoming much too fond of her. Especially when he got on to the subject of his next transfer, expected within six months or a year, and how he could probably negotiate a relatively civilised posting, should he decide it was necessary. He was angling, working up to a proposal, and both of them knew it. But only Seana knew how futile it would be, and she couldn't quite find the words to explain.

She liked Ralph, really liked him. They could talk about almost everything, and often did. He was pleasant, easy company, with none of the emotional ups and downs she seemed to have experienced in Ryan. But she couldn't love him, and were it not for her loneliness, would have told him so long before.

There was one subject—apart from Ryan—that Seana also never mentioned to Ralph, or even to Mrs

Jorgensen, who also managed the occasional visit. The white moose, she decided, would be *her* secret, despite the fact she couldn't ignore the fact of sharing it with Ryan.

And two days after Ralph's latest visit, she wished that she had mentioned the animal, now shed of its antler velvet and carrying an enormous rack of ebony antlers. A helicopter fire patrol, flying between her tower and Mike's lookout to the west, broke suddenly into the radio chatter with a startled report of spotting the big white moose, and it seemed that the word spread instantly throughout the whole of Alberta.

It wasn't yet hunting season, but Seana's tower road swarmed with intending hunters, all greedily hoping for a sight of the rare animal.

Demands for use of her tower became a thrice-daily occurrence, and she was occasionally subjected to streams of verbal abuse for her continuing refusal. She thought of reporting the worst instance, when a hulking youth climbed halfway up the tower making definite threats, but there was nobody to spare in the incessant fire alert to help her anyway.

'Besides,' she told herself that evening, after carefully locking herself inside the cabin, 'the last thing I want is Frank Hutton to start having second thoughts about letting me have the job. He'd fire me as soon as look at me, and with the greatest of personal pleasure.'

Another problem laid at Ryan Stranger's door; of course the forestry superintendent had heard about the incident at the dance, so Ryan's protests about Seana no longer had any inverse effect on Hutton's opinions.

Where the would-be hunters were concerned, Seana took the course of least resistance. She lied, blatantly and without a qualm. She denied ever having seen the moose and even invented long-winded stories to make her conviction seem more valid.

She almost came a cropper when the moose walked right across the tower road, not a quarter of a mile in front of an approaching vehicle. Fortunately it was hidden by a fold in the track, but Seana had difficulty holding back a giggle when she denied for the thousandth time having ever seen it.

In addition to lying, she started praying for rain. Rain, she knew, would not only reduce the growing fire danger, a danger that would increase tenfold with a forest full of hunters, but which she hoped would make her road sufficiently treacherous that nobody could reach her anyway. If the moose understood her prayers, she couldn't know, but she started seeing it almost daily, often uncomfortably close to either tower clearing or road.

And sooner or later, she realised, some hunter or another pilot would spot the beast, not only confirming her deceit but bringing increased throngs of hunters to the area. There was only one chance of salvation—the ominous, steel-grey thunderheads that had begun building on the western horizon each evening.

Yet her prayers seemed in vain. The storm clouds would swim over the Rocky Mountains far to the west, hover menacingly through the vivid sunsets created by the dust and smoke of the fires which burned in virtually every forest district, then withdraw in a drumroll of thunder and flashing sheets of heat lightning, fire from the sky which luckily stayed far enough above the parched forests to avoid starting even more fires.

And then, one night when even the shaded cabin squatted for shelter beneath the spreading pines, her prayers were answered with a vengeance. She watched the dark, glowering clouds build up through the day, looming closer and closer and visibly dumping rain as they moved across from British Columbia. The forestry radio operator, jubilation in her voice, reported inches of rain on the B.C. side, and at four o'clock Mike howled his delight that the rain had started over his Saddle Hills tower.

'But there's a lot of lightning,' he shouted over the drumming of the rain on his cabin roof. 'Seana, you make sure you . . .' His voice was drowned in a sudden crackle of static, then the thunder began at White Mountain Tower, and Seana's radio packed up completely as the lightning marched across.

From her viewpoint on the tower, she watched the cloud bank roll towards her from the west like a huge, living grey tidal wave. The top of the cloud, at first, was below her line of sight; she could actually see the setting sun above the violence of the storm. But as the cloud drew closer, the rising contours of the land forced it upwards again, and suddenly Seana realised the cloud was spitting lightning all around her. Afraid, she turned to open the trapdoor to her ladder, but was immediately thrust back as the winds arrived to shake the tower and slam through the trapdoor in vicious gusts.

Afraid to risk the wet, now slippery ladder, she turned once again to her radio, but the shattering lightning caused such static she could get no response. Looking out, she could see only the angry sea of cloud, now moving like something from a horror movie. The spurts of lightning which had appeared so dramatically lovely when she was above them now turned to malevolent serpents as they struck at the ground, narrowly missing the natural lightning rod of the tower.

She was almost sick with fear, mostly because she had no options. It was useless to suddenly remember the standing orders to abandon the tower in any electrical storm; she'd forgotten, and now it was far too late to change her mind.

A sudden, flashing *twang* drew her eyes as a chain of

lightning snaked down one of the tower's stabilising cables, and the air was immediately rank with cordite, the smell of death too close for comfort.

To try and descend the ladder now would be foolhardy in the extreme, but dared she stay, perched as she was on the highest point for twenty miles around? On a perfect lightning rod? Once again she struggled with the trapdoor, peering through the rain-slicked web of steel that led to the ground and possible safety. Her mind was numb, empty of conscious thought as she stared dizzily downward to where the thirsty clay sucked up the rain almost as fast as it fell.

She was about to chance it, had one foot through the trapdoor, when another bolt of lightning slithered down the guy-wire, crackling sparks against the circular cage around the ladder. Seana withdrew, suddenly sobered by the utter absurdity of her actions. Outside there was only the unending sea of cloud, shot with deadly bolts of lightning and the occasional wash of sheet lightning that lit up the entire sky like flashes of Aurora Borealis, the Northern Lights.

A sudden gust of intense wind flung the tiny cupola about, and Seana noticed her binoculars as they skittered towards the edge of the sighting table. She reached for them, and as her fingers closed on the strap there was a mighty crash of thunder right in the cupola with her and the sky was on fire. She lost her balance and fell to the wooden floor, where she lay shivering in a foetal curve, her every nerve straining with stark, primaeval fear and her eyes shut tightly. Around her, the sky writhed with lightning fires, with occasional sizzling serpents that slithered across the roof and down the steel structure. But she saw none of it.

Mercifully, she sank into an oblivion of unconsciousness that lasted until the storm centre passed. She came out of it confused, still afraid, and with the

vaguest awareness of someone calling her name from
far, far away. The binoculars lay beside her on the
floor, miraculously unbroken, and on the sighting table
the radio continued to combine short bursts of clarity
with long intervals of static. As she struggled to her
feet, Seana realised the storm centre now was to the
east of her, and the lightning was no longer striking
near her tower.

'Seana! Seanaaa . . .'

She heard the call, and in her confusion hurried to
peer through the rainwashed windows, but she could
see nothing through the darkness.

'Seana!' And this time she realised the source, but
even as she moved towards the trapdoor it was thrust
open to reveal a mop of carroty hair, streaming with
water, and the brilliant green eyes of Ryan Stranger.

He surged through, slamming the door behind him
and standing on it against the pressures of the wind.
His eyes, just for an instant, she thought, seemed soft
with concern. But only for an instant; then they
underwent a subtle colour change to regain the mocking brilliance she was more accustomed to.

'Well, you're all right after all.' It wasn't a question;
it was an accusation, almost. At best some form of frank
condemnation.

'I . . . yes,' she finally stammered without much conviction—and became aware of how weak were her legs,
how tremulous her stomach. Moving to the observer's
chair, she sank into it, turning her eyes away from his
accusing gaze and staring abstractedly out to the darkness of the clouds.

'Are you strong enough to climb down from here, or
do I have to carry you? There'll be more lightning
soon; we have to get out of it quickly.'

His abrasive voice stirred something within her,
some final shred of dignity untouched by her fears. 'Of

course I'm strong enough!' she snapped.

'Good. Then let's go,' he replied, and without another word he flung open the trap and stepped
through, moving with infinite caution on the slippery,
soaking ladder. Seana followed, all too aware that his
attention was divided between herself and his climbing,
a dangerous risk.

It seemed to take forever to reach the ground, and
she was shivering with a combination of fear, cold and
wet long before she slumped from the final step into
Ryan's waiting arms.

He didn't ask permission, but lifted her unprotest-
ingly and slithered through the greasy mud to the cabin
porch, where he had to set her down long enough to
take her key and fumble open the door. The darkness
inside was absolute, but in a flicker of distant lightning
he found his way to the nearest chair and gently deposited her into it.

'Stay there,' he muttered, and she could do nothing
but obey. Her trembling legs wouldn't have supported
her.

Reaching for her matches on the kitchen table, he
first lit the pressure lamp, then threw small wood and
large into the airtight heater, added a drop of kerosene
and threw in a lighted match. The fire took hold in a
muffled *whoof* that startled Seana with its suddenness.

'Now, let's get you into something dry,' he said,
taking her gently by one hand and drawing her to her
feet. Seana's first reaction was to resist, but her
strength had deserted her in her terror; she stood
meekly as he stripped her to the skin and began briskly
rubbing her body with a towel he had found.

He picked up her sleeping bag, looked at it for a
moment, then discarded it in favour of a blanket she
had begun using as the nights became warmer.
Wrapping her in the blanket so tightly she could hardly

breathe, he plumped her into a chair near the now-glowing heater and began drying her hair, not being especially gentle about it.

When she winced, he muttered something that might have been an apology, then stopped long enough to search the cupboards for two glasses. Jerking a bottle of brandy from his jacket pocket, he half-filled each glass and held one to her lips.

'Slowly,' he cautioned, 'but drink it all; it'll warm you up quicker.'

Easier said than done, she found, and finally had to wriggle one arm free so she held the glass herself. Ryan merely shook his head and reached down to tuck the blanket more securely over her bared shoulder.

Then, rather to her surprise, he padded over to her dressing table and picked up her hairbrush. She sat there as if in a dream, slowly sipping the brandy while Ryan worked the brush through her hair with a gentleness equal to what she herself might have managed. As he did so, he seemed to be crooning softly, as if he were grooming a horse, but instead of finding the comparison offensive, Seana found it strangely relaxing.

When her hair was brushed into a smooth tide that crackled with the electricity in the damp air, Ryan noticed the glass was finally empty, so he filled it again and handed it back to her.

'Are you hungry? Or could you at least eat something?'

She nodded, not ready to trust her now warm but still trembling body.

'Right. Stay there and work on that; I'll find something.'

And she obeyed, without thinking to object, only half aware of his movements as he paced through the cabin, turning on the stove, opening cans and stirring things.

It wasn't until he had placed a bowl of steaming broth in her hands that the smell of food combined with the growing warmth inside to create hunger. She worked at it slowly, tasting each morsel and savouring the flavour, feeling herself come to life again.

Ryan picked up a bowl of his own and paced catlike, almost nervously, as he ate it, and Seana realised for the first time that he was leaving puddles behind him with every step.

'You . . . you're all wet,' she protested, half rising from the chair, only to meet a firm hand that thrust her back down.

'I've been wet before,' he replied, voice heavy with sarcasm. 'I'm not made of sugar; it won't kill me.' Then he grinned. 'Besides, I doubt if there are any dry clothes here that would fit me.'

'Well, you could wrap up in this,' she snapped, almost flinging away the blanket before she remembered she was naked beneath it. For some inexplicable reason that angered her, and she continued in a tone of voice that might only have been described as shrewish, 'or would you rather be all macho and strong and wind up with pneumonia?'

Ryan laughed at her, his teeth white in the glow of the pressure lamp as he threw back his head. 'Yep . . . you're better,' he said sarcastically. 'Right back to normal and bossy as always.'

Padding lithely over to where he'd dumped her towel on a nail in the cabin wall, he whipped it over his soaking hair, then shrugged out of the denim jacket and the waterlogged shirt beneath it. Towelling himself briskly, he shifted over closer to the heater, finally sprawling into a chair and propping up his feet so that the warmth drew clouds of steam from his wet moccasins and filled the room with their pungent, smoky odour.

Seana finished off the broth, whereupon he fetched her a third tot of brandy and insisted she sip at it. Then he began once again to prowl about the room. She couldn't help but be aware of his lean, half-naked body, especially after he turned out the pressure lamp to leave them with only the glow of the fire for light. The flames cast an entrancing shadow pattern across the rippling muscles as he moved.

'I do suppose you're aware you could have been killed today,' he said finally. 'What in hell ever possessed you to stay up there with an electrical storm coming? Have you got a death wish or something?'

There was a curious harshness in his voice, but it was nonetheless softly quiet against the snapping and crackling of the fire and the rumble of thunder outside.

'I . . . I didn't think of it in time,' she replied. 'Mike tried to warn me, I think, but then the radio . . .'

Ryan cut her off with a brief, curt gesture.

'Never mind the excuses. Didn't you ever hear of just plain common sense?' Damn it, it's one of the first things they teach you. When there's an electrical storm you get out of the tower—the bloody thing's a natural lightning rod, for God's sake! The fact that you're still alive proves you really must have more luck than brains.'

His tone angered her, but even worse was the fact that he was so obviously right. But so damnably condescending about it . . .

'Well, nobody asked you to worry about me, did they?' she snapped petulantly.

'*Somebody's* got to. You aren't safe to leave alone for five minutes. God! I'm surprised you survived long enough to grow up.'

'I've managed well enough without your interference so far,' she cried angrily.

'Like I said: more luck than brains,' Ryan replied grimly.

It was too much—far too much, on top of her ordeal of terror on top of the tower. Seana felt the tears coming and hated herself, but she couldn't stop them.

'Oh, get out of here, then!' she stormed. 'Get out, and don't ever . . . ever come back! All you ever do is shout at me and . . . and . . .' The rest was lost in the rush of choking sobs that racked her slim body.

'Typical bloody woman! Start losing the argument and you have to cry,' he replied, only now his voice was gentle, strangely comforting as he gathered her into his arms, blanket and all, and carried her to her bed.

The blanket was whipped from her unresisting body, but before she could even think to object, he had slipped her into the warm, down-filled cocoon of her sleeping bag and zipped it round her.

'Now stop your blubbering and go to sleep,' he muttered, bending to plant a soft, passionless kiss on her forehead and then returning to his chair by the fire.

It was done so . . . so paternalistically that Seana found her tears giving way to something that was closer to indignation than true anger, and as the warmth of the sleeping bag melted around her, a comfortable lassitude set in as well.

'You're not . . . not very sympathetic at all,' she muttered, half to herself but not caring if he heard her or not.

'Shut up and go to sleep,' he retorted softly, still without any real anger in his voice. 'The last thing you need right now is sympathy.'

Seana didn't reply, but obediently closed her eyes

and tried to obey his command. Now that she was warm and comfortable, the terrors of her ordeal seemed to diminish, despite the renewed assault of thunder and lightning outside the snugness of the cabin.

It was some time later, how long she didn't know, that she peeped through half-open eyes to see him standing naked before the slow-banked fire, scrubbing his body into a glowing warmth that complemented the strong muscles now only too evident. She stared unashamedly, but when he turned in her direction she closed her eyes and pretended to be still asleep.

When next she looked, he was wrapped in her blanket, his clothing strung on a makeshift line above the heater and his strong body relaxed in the cabin's only decent chair.

'You can't sleep there,' she murmured sleepily, only half aware that she was speaking. 'You'll get a stiff neck.'

'Is that some kind of invitation, ladybug?' he asked softly. 'And be careful how you answer; I just might accept and you'd end up with more than you bargained for.'

She'd already closed her eyes again. Now she determined to keep her mouth shut as well. How could she possibly reply to such a provocative question? Certainly, she realised despite being half asleep, not by telling him the truth.

But she didn't have to open her eyes to know that he'd left his chair and come to stand beside her, and a moment later to *lie* beside her, still wrapped in the blanket.

His lips nuzzled her ear and he whispered to her, softly as thistle down, 'You're a fraud . . . do you know that?'

But he didn't really want an answer, she knew, and in moments he was breathing slowly and deeply, un-

aware of how much his nearness was affecting Seana's
peace of mind.

What would he do, she wondered, if she woke him
now, woke him with kisses, woke him by caressing his
magnificent body with her hands, her lips? Would he
turn to her, give her the love she needed so very badly,
or would he turn away, rejecting her? She was asleep
herself before she could decide.

Two things impressed themselves upon her mind as
she struggled out of sleep next morning. One was the
smell of coffee, the other was the haunting, wild
melody of a bull elk singing his mating, fighting challenge somewhere in the distance. The strange, eerie
whistling bugle sounded unreal, like something created
by a sound-effects specialist instead of a living, breathing animal.

Seana languished a moment, letting the haunting
melody imprint itself in her mind, idly wishing she had a
tape recorder. Then reality brought her stark upright in
the bed, clutching the sleeping bag around her naked-
ness as she peered around the cabin for Ryan.

But she was alone, and yet the bubbling coffee pro-
claimed another presence, confirming her scattered
memories of the night before. Had he really slept in
the same bed with her? She couldn't quite bring herself
to think rationally about his necessary stripping of her
body, his amazingly sensual brushing of her hair.

She looked out the window, surprised to find that it
wasn't even quite dawn, although an almost imperceptible greying of the sky combined with the shriek
of a whisky-jack to announce the sun's imminent arrival. Seana lay back for a moment, then scrambled
out of bed, grabbing up her now-dry clothing and hurry-
ing into it.

Looking out of the window, she saw nothing but
Ryan's truck to confirm that he was still somewhere

about, despite the tangible evidence of memory and coffee pot. It was at that moment she became aware of the pre-dawn silence and realised just how early it really was, for the forestry radio to be without its usual crackling comfort.

She cast her mind back to the previous evening, blushing at the memory of how Ryan had so casually and competently dealt with her own, memorably vivid, incompetence. The memories were embarrassing, yet somehow very tender and pleasant.

But where was he? Then, as if in answer, she saw a tiny figure emerge from the tower cupola and descend the ladder with startling haste.

'Well, you look a little brighter this morning,' he announced through a cheerful grin as he entered the cabin. 'Did you wake up early enough to hear that old bull elk a few minutes ago ... and if you did, how come my coffee isn't poured yet?'

Seana didn't get a chance to reply. Obviously in a chipper and happy mood, he never gave her a chance. 'Big fellow, from the sound of him,' he said. 'The elk should be moving through here pretty soon on their way west, but you'll have to start getting up in the morning if you want to see them. You might get a decent look from the tower, although they'll probably avoid the clearing, especially after tomorrow. They'll either cross just down that first ridge, or over behind us in the jackpines, where the hunters can't get at them so easily.'

'Hunters ...' It was half a question and half an answer, but he didn't take up the answer.

'Season opens tomorrow, don't forget, and this place will seem like a battlefield for the first few days.'

He wandered over to pour them both some coffee, one raised eyebrow chastising Seana for not having done so at his earlier suggestion, then stood fondling the cup in his hands for a moment before he said anything more. Seana watched his fingers, thinking of them in that same sensuous motion at the small of her back, and felt her pulse begin to race.

'Mrs Jorgensen will be over some time tomorrow, provided the road holds up,' he said then. 'So at least you'll have some moral support to help you through the worst of it. I wouldn't expect you to have any trouble, normally, but now they've found out about my white moose, anything's possible. I'd stay over myself, if I could, but that's ... not really possible. Anyway, you'll be okay with Mother Jorgensen. Anybody crazy enough to tangle with her is likely to get a rifle barrel wrapped around his head!'

Seana chuckled at the mental picture of Mrs Jorgensen defending her against the gun-toting hordes, but Ryan's face showed no humour. He was deadly serious.

'Just remember that there's a law against people shooting anywhere near the tower, so see that you enforce it. Anybody so much as gives you any back-talk, you get on the radio and somebody'll be up to straighten them up.'

'You're really convinced I'm incompetent, aren't you?' she asked then, suddenly, unaccountably angry at being treated like a child. Forgotten was the turmoil and terror of the night before, the earlier incidents in which Ryan's help had been crucial. 'What right do you have to go arranging my life all the time?' she cried. 'Don't any of you think I can manage without a nursemaid?'

'You don't really want me to answer that,' he growled.

'Yes! Yes, I do,' she snapped in reply. 'I would remind you that I've managed quite nicely for months without any help.'

'Sure you have, apart from trying to burn down the cabin, or electrocute yourself,' he replied with a sneer. 'God knows what you get up to when I'm not around, but . . .'

'But nothing! That's the whole point—the only time I have problems is when you *are* around,' Seana raged. 'You may think I'm a walking disaster area, but let me tell you, Ryan Stranger—you're a jinx, which is even worse. And you can't convince me that this week-end will be one bit worse than the past two weeks has been. You can't imagine the hassles I've had with people wanting to climb the tower and look for our moose . . .'

She broke off lamely, suddenly realising what she'd said and how he might take it, but Ryan apparently didn't notice the joint reference, or ignored it.

'It'll be ten times as bad,' he scowled. 'I could kill that damn chopper pilot, with his big mouth! Every yahoo from here to Calgary will be up here tomorrow looking for that moose, and the dumb animal is too stupid to realise it. I saw him from the tower this morning, not a mile away, wandering around like he owned the country. And he stands out so damned clearly, which is what worries me. You couldn't miss him from the air . . .'

He broke off suddenly, and for a moment stared angrily into his coffee cup. 'Listen,' he said then, and there could be no doubt about his seriousness. 'If you see anybody . . . *anybody* flying any kind of aircraft around here, I want you on the radio immediately. Is that clear? It's against the law to spot game from the air, but somebody'll try it, sure as hell.'

Then he glanced at his wristwatch and suddenly leapt to his feet.

'Damn,' he muttered. 'I'd like to have stayed longer, ladybug, but I've got a party flying in tonight, and I'm nowhere near ready for them. If I don't get the lead out, I'll find myself out of business before the season even starts.'

It was at that instant that his seasonal profession as a big game guide became a reality to Seana, and with it the sickening suspicion that immediately found a vocal outlet.

'That's why you're so concerned about the moose!' she exclaimed, eyes wide with horror. 'You want him for yourself . . . or for one of your . . . clients. Oh, how could you?'

She thought for a moment she was going to be sick. The thought that Ryan could . . . *would* shoot the animal that she had allowed to become a symbol of her feelings for him was too much to bear. Her accusation drew from Ryan, however, a look that was first confused, then scornfully angry.

'Well, of course,' he replied. 'He's mine. He's always *been* mine. I've just been waiting until he was big enough to have a decent set of antlers to match that rare white hide.'

Ryan turned and shouldered his way to the door before Seana could reply, shouting back over his shoulder: 'They're calling you on the radio.'

He was gone before she could say a word, so she answered the radio instead, officially beginning her last day of peace and quiet on White Mountain Tower.

CHAPTER SIX

'WHAT the devil have you and Ryan been fighting about this time? He just about ran me off the road a few minutes ago, driving like a total damned fool and with a scowl on his face like I've never seen.'

It was typical of Mrs Jorgensen that she didn't bother with traditional greetings, despite having arrived a full day early, but Seana was in no mood to be polite.

'If you're going to stay here and babysit me all weekend, please have the decency not to mention that man's name again,' she snapped. 'Not today, not tomorrow, not ever!'

'All right. Shall we have coffee before I unload the car, or after?' Seana's friend replied with a knowing shake of her head.

'Oh . . . I'm sorry, Mrs J. It's just that . . . he . . . oh, he makes me so mad I could spit!' Seana replied. 'Come on and I'll help you with the car; then we can sit down and enjoy our coffee in peace.'

Together, they unloaded bags of fresh meat, bread and other goodies, then sat down to the coffee, still hardly cooled since Ryan's precipitate departure.

'You're not supposed to be here until tomorrow, I thought,' Seana said. 'Not that I'd believe anything that man told me anyway, but . . .'

'Ry . . . that man told you the truth as much as he knew,' Mrs Jorgensen replied. 'I was going to come up in the morning, but there's heavy rain forecast again, and I really don't think much of your road when it's

wet, so I took a day off they owed me and came early.
I hope you don't mind.'

'Oh, of course not. I'm just a bit shirty with . . . you
know who, that's all.'

'Yes, I rather gathered that much,' was the dry
retort. 'But from the bit I saw of him, you must have
given as good as you got. Not that I expect you to tell
me about it, of course . . .'

'Not *much* you don't,' chuckled Seana, her humour
regaining itself in the pleasure of the older woman's
company. She vividly related the events of the evening
before, and while she avoided mentioning who had
slept where, she couldn't very well deny that Ryan had
spent the night. Even as she told the story, which
became increasingly humorous, in retrospect, she
didn't really know if she expected Mrs Jorgensen to be
horrified, shocked, amused, or just what.

'You're a fool, and I'm sure he told you so,' the
older woman raged when Seana had finished. 'I'm not
surprised he was angry, hearing you tell it your way.
Damn it, Seana, you've no idea how lucky you are.'

'Oh, yes, I do. And I'm sorry to have sounded flip-
pant, because I know it wasn't funny. It was terrifying,
really, and of course I was lucky.'

'You don't know *how* lucky. There was a fellow on
Bald Mountain Tower a couple of years back who had
a lightning bolt go right through the cupola, down the
tower steel, smash through his generator shack and half
rip the door off his outhouse. He'd have been nothing
but a cinder if he'd been in the tower at the time, and
as it was, he gave up being a towerman that very day.'

'I can understand why,' Seana replied. 'Even being
in his cabin, it must have been a frightful thing to
watch. I know how frightened I was, at least until I
fainted.'

She thought at first that Mrs Jorgensen's peal of

laughter was directed at herself, until she heard the words that tumbled out with it.

'Oh, he wasn't in the . . . the tower,' Mrs Jorgensen gasped. 'He was . . . in the outhouse when it happened . . . and he stayed there until the storm was over, too.'

Seana found herself joining in the laughter, but the joke was too close to her own experience to be *that* funny. Both women, nonetheless, were still chuckling when there was an imperious knock on the door.

'Where the hell's this white moose everyone's talking about?' The speaker was a small, chubby man whose voice and stance indicated that he was at least well on the way to being falling-down drunk.

Seana was aghast, considering the time of day, and she stood silent a moment, wondering what she could or should say to the man.

'Hummph! Won't tell me, eh? Well, doesn't matter. I'll just climb up and have a look for myself,' he muttered, turning away to track a weaving path towards the base of the tower.

'He'll kill himself!' Seana exclaimed, then flashed out of the door and managed to grab the man by the jacket before he could start his climb.

'You can't go up there,' she panted. 'I can't let you; it's against regulations. I'd get fired!' Her voice was coming in uneven bursts as her mind struggled to recall every possible argument against the man's stated intention.

She was prepared for argument, but not for the sudden shove he gave her, a push that forced her several steps backward and almost knocked her sprawling in the wet grass.

'I'm a taxpayer, and my paying . . . my taxes pay your wages, lady, so just get out of my way!' he snarled in a slurred drawl, stepping on to the first rung of the ladder. Seana stood there, speechless with impotent anger.

She watched as the man climbed two more rungs, then cried out in alarm as the shattering roar of a shotgun boomed through the clearing.

'You be down out of there in two seconds or you'll get the next one where it'll hurt the most,' Mrs Jorgensen said in a quiet, deadly voice. Seana turned to find her friend standing in a careless pose, the muzzle of a pump-action shotgun pointed casually at the base of the tower. Suddenly sober, the man was on the ground and headed for his vehicle before the time was up.

'Well, that's one less to worry about tomorrow,' Mrs Jorgensen said coolly, unloading the shotgun and leaning it handy to the cabin door. 'Now let's go and finish our coffee.' She brushed aside Seana's startled exclamations with a brittle laugh. 'When you get to my age, dear, you'll realise when it's time for action instead of talk. No big deal.'

But Seana noticed her hands were trembling, just a little, as Mrs Jorgensen stirred more sugar into her coffee with over-elaborate casualness.

As the day progressed, they had several other visitors despite the arrival of the forecast rains. Only one was welcome and both women cried out with delight at his arrival.

'You should have shot the bastard,' Ralph Beatty said when he was told, in explicit and extensive detail, about Mrs Jorgensen's exploits. 'He's just lucky neither Ryan nor I were here, or he'd be in worse shape than just having a bit of buckshot in his breeches.'

'Hardly buckshot, Ralph. You know I only keep the gun for partridges,' Mrs Jorgensen said.

'And I for one would like to change the subject,' said Seana. She couldn't very well insist that Ralph not mention Ryan, but the thought of being rescued yet again by the red-bearded bushman was not to be contemplated.

'Oh, all right,' Ralph replied grumpily. 'If you don't want to talk about anything exciting, I might as well go out to the truck and get your present, before I forget. But I'm not sure it's me who should be delivering it. I'm supposed to be able to foil the competition, not aid and abet him!'

He returned a minute later with a small plastic-covered parcel which he handed to Seana with an exaggerated flourish.

'Compliments of one Ryan Stranger, who says you're to wear it each and every time you leave this cabin, no matter what the time or reason. It will protect you, he hopes, against idiots like the one you fixed up so nicely this morning.' Then he grinned ruefully. 'Damn Ryan anyway; he always did have all the best ideas. I just wish this one had been mine.'

Inside the package was a folded plastic slicker, but a slicker of such a brilliant, eye-shattering, glaring, fluorescent blazing orange it was painful to look at.

'Does he really expect me to wear this thing?' Seana cried in half-angry disbelief. 'Heavens I can't even stand to *look* at it!'

'He does ... and I do ... and Mrs Jorgensen does,' was the deliberate, unarguable reply.

'Well, I suppose it's better than being mistaken for a moose,' said Seana in a vain attempt to lighten the atmosphere.

'It isn't funny,' Ralph told her. 'Nothing that moves is safe out there, especially at weekends. You'll wear it and like it. Understood?'

'Yes, sir. Anything you say, sir,' she replied. 'I suppose I'll have to, because of course we wouldn't want to upset Ryan Stranger, would we?'

'Not unless you want to be paddled where our

would-be hunter almost got shot,' Mrs Jorgensen interjected. 'And I'd help hold you down, too, young lady. Not that Ryan would need any help, I imagine.'

'Neither would I,' Ralph put in grimly. 'And don't you forget it, Seana, or you'll definitely be sorry.'

'All right, that's enough. I promise to wear the wretched thing,' Seana sighed. 'Even if it makes me feel like a school patrol, it's better than the punishment you three would come up with!'

With that issue settled, Ralph finished his coffee and departed on his rounds, and the remainder of the day was fairly quiet. It wasn't until they sat down to their evening meal that Mrs Jorgensen's increasing nervousness really began to register, and at first Seana thought it was merely a reaction from the morning's incident. She was quite surprised, therefore, to find upon asking that her friend had something quite different worrying her.

'I've got a sort of a proposition for you,' the older woman began tentatively, 'and although I'd like an answer fairly soon, so that I can make the arrangements, I can understand why you might not want to rush into any decision.

'What I'm thinking is this; I'd like to take a trip to Denmark, where I was born, and see what few relations I still have over there. But it would mean leaving the house empty and maybe even giving up my job. Unless you'll help.'

'Well, of course, I'll do anything I can,' Seana told her. 'But I don't see . . .'

'I want you to take over both—house and job.'

The answer was so unexpected, so unusual, that Seana had to catch her breath. Obviously her friend had given the matter great consideration, but . . .

'I . . . I really don't know what to say,' she replied finally. 'I mean . . . I could handle the house, but the job? What would Frank Hutton think? I can't imagine him going along with it.'

'Have you got anything better to do?' It was a typical Mrs Jorgensen approach, direct and to the point.

'Well . . . er . . . no. But I don't know when *this* job will be over. I mean, it could be next week if we get enough rain, or it could be going right through October if it gets dry again. But of course you know that.'

'Not a problem; I wasn't thinking of leaving until November.'

Seana laughed nervously. 'You've really got it all figured out,' she said. 'I don't even know why you bothered to ask, in fact. You might as well have pulled a Ryan Stranger approach, and just told me.'

It was, she realised immediately she'd said it, quite the wrong thing to have said. Despite her crusty, competent exterior, Mrs Jorgensen was easily as sensitive as Seana herself, and the remark had clearly hurt.

'Oh, I'm sorry; I shouldn't have said that, and I honestly didn't mean it,' Seana sighed. 'It's just that . . . well, Ryan makes such a habit of trying to organise my life as if I were a child . . . oh, I guess I'm just all mixed up. Of course I'll do it for you, provided of course you can wangle Frank Hutton into agreeing.'

It looked for an instant as if her friend was about to cry. The soft blue eyes grew even softer as relief poured into them. 'I'm glad,' Mrs Jorgensen said quietly, 'but let's not talk about it any more now. There'll be time in the morning, and you'll have had time to sleep on it.'

By morning, a glorious, cloudy, drizzly morning that promised even heavier rain as the day progressed, Seana was doubly sure that accepting Mrs Jorgensen's proposal was a good idea.'

'Good,' said Mrs J. when Seana voiced her decision. 'Now off you go and play towerman. I'm going to just clean up these few dishes and then I want to see about some nice fat grouse for lunch.'

Seana felt much better about it all, and she scampered up the long ladder like a happy squirrel. not even breathing hard when she finally reached the top.

The view was magnificent, until she glanced down at a willow thicket not half a mile from the cabin and saw with alarm the white moose ... her moose ... savagely shaking his enormous antlers. Grabbing up the binoculars, Seana could see the leaves and bark flying everywhere as the animal lunged and slashed and lunged again. She almost believed she could hear his angry grunts as he polished his antlers in preparation for the battles ahead.

Shorn of their velvet, the moose's antlers were an ebony black in the daylight, and as she watched longer, she realised he wasn't fully into his rutting season, but was only playing with the willow thicket, testing his strength and cleaning the last shreds of dried velvet from his antlers. She watched for several minutes, then did a thorough scan of the area to see if there were any hunters who might present danger to the animal.

No worries; they were all driving up and down the tower road, but the only person she could see on foot was Mrs Jorgensen, safely clad in red as she stalked her luncheon of grouse.

Seana looked once more at the moose, her mind shifting to Ryan and his claim on the animal. 'Well, we'll see about that, too,' she muttered to herself. Unable to forget the magical occasion when she and Ryan had shared the moose's ethereal majesty, she found his claim maddening, infuriating.

How could Ryan possibly be so insensitive? Or, she wondered, was she reading far too much into one episode in a relationship that had since been anything but peaceful?

It was approaching noon, and Seana was seriously thinking about lunch when she looked down to see Mrs Jorgensen slowly walking up the tower road with several ruffed grouse slung over one shoulder. And she hadn't even heard the shots, 'Which says a lot about my powers of observation,' she muttered to herself.

The woman's scarlet tunic made her movements easy to follow, although she periodically disappeared from sight owing to twists and turns in the road. Concentrating as she was on the red jacket, Seana didn't consciously notice, at first, the silvery-brown shape that occasionally came into view several hundred metres behind Mrs Jorgensen, paralleling her path but staying in the brush beside the road.

And when she did notice, her first reaction was that it must be a dog . . . until she used the binoculars and saw the animal's peculiar, distinctive, rolling stride.

'Oh, my God!' she gasped as recognition dawned. Then she flew to push open one of the tower's hinged windows.

'Mrs J! Mrs Jorgensen!' she shouted, 'Oh . . . oh . . . look. *Look!* Behind you . . .'

Her friend looked up and waved a cheery greeting, then pointed to the grouse she was carrying. Obviously she had heard Seana call, but hadn't picked out the words.

Seana screamed . . . as loudly as she could, this time. 'Behind you! A bear . . . *a bear*!'

This time the message got through. Mrs Jorgensen turned with her shotgun at the ready, and although Seana could no longer see the bear, she realised that Mrs Jorgensen was properly warned and would be alert. Turning, she flung open the trapdoor and scurried down the ladder, still shouting encouragement and advice.

The two women reached the cabin door together, but with no sign of the ominous follower.

'Well,' said Mrs Jorgensen, 'I'm not real happy about that!'

She had caught only a glimpse of the bear, which had seemed to take fright from Seana's screams, but went on to explain that the bear hadn't seemed nearly frightened enough.

'Any bear out here that isn't mortally afraid of just the *smell* of a human is a damned dangerous animal. It's different in the national parks, where they get too used to people and where damned fools feed them despite the warnings, but out here the bear should be first to run, unless it's a female with cubs ... or a grizzly.'

They compared notes on the animal's description, and Mrs Jorgensen became even more convinced it might be a young, roving grizzly. So they spent the afternoon rigging a complicated system of tin cans on string, hanging cans from the eaves, from bushes all round the cabin, and even on the porch itself.

Neither of them had been able to face lunch, but they savoured the grouse at dinner time, wrapped in bacon and gently roasted to succulent tenderness.

There was no further sign of the bear, but when it finally came time for Mrs Jorgensen to return home, she insisted on leaving the shotgun, complete with several loads of double-O buckshot she found in her game bag.

'I'll feel safer just knowing you've got it,' she said on departing. 'I'm not sure it'll be needed and I hope it isn't, and for goodness' sake make sure you don't go shooting Ryan if you get into another fight with him. It's for bears, dear, not wolves!'

But as the days passed, Seana found no use for the shotgun at all, although she was forced to admit the bear had her thoroughly spooked. Not a day passed without her seeing the animal, although always at some distance and always from the safety of the tower.

But at night! Only the wind ever stirred her tin can warning system, but the bear was out there . . . she could feel it. And when she was halfway down the ladder at lunch-time on the following Friday, a chance look downward almost shocked her into losing her grip on the cold steel rungs.

The bear was almost beneath her, nearly close enough to touch as it nosed curiously around the front of her car.

'Hey, get out of there! G'wan . . . shoo, bear!'

She shouted and screamed and finally cried with frustration because the animal totally ignored her. It did peer weakly about when she screamed, but either could not or would not comprehend where the noises were coming from. Finally Seana climbed back up into the tower, where she grabbed up an empty soft drink tin and flung it at the animal.

The bear gave a hoarse grunt and danced sideways when the can struck it on the rump after glancing off the hood of the car, but then he resumed his prowling survey of the car and wandered up on to the cabin porch.

'A fat lot of good that did,' Seana muttered as the bear ploughed through the dangling tin cans without so much as a flinch. Clearly her warning system had provided only false security, and that thought made her decidedly frightened.

Deciding that discretion, in this case, most definitely was the better part of valour, she lost no time getting on the radio to relay her dilemma. The response, while overwhelming, was discouragingly frivolous from most quarters.

'Go down and kick him in the rump,' came the response from Torrens Tower.

'Put salt on his tail,' laughed an unidentifiable

ranger in his truck somewhere to the south.

Only Dick Fisher, dear, reliable Dick, had any really constructive advice, and even that didn't do much to improve Seana's ragged temper. 'You just stay in the tower,' he said. 'Ryan Stranger's going to drop by this evening and he'll take care of it.'

'Oh, that's just great,' Seana replied. 'And what am I supposed to do in the meantime, starve. What if he tries to break into the cabin? Do I offer him half my lunch?'

Disgusted, she slammed off the radio amidst cheers from the many other listeners, idly wondering as she did so why Ryan hadn't come on the radio himself. At the very least he might have checked to see if visitors were welcome.

But as the bear kept her treed in the tower throughout the afternoon, she decided even Ryan's presence would be a distinct comfort. The whole thing became something of a game, though not without its sobering moments.

The bear would disappear out of Seana's field of vision, so after a while she would start down the ladder with some vague idea of making a dash for the cabin. But as soon as she reached the ground, the bear would reappear, usually where she least expected him. It never made any attempt to charge her, but would simply stand and stare at her while she scurried back up the ladder, screaming with frustrated rage. It happened five times before she finally realised the stupidity of it all and gave up.

'Damn Ryan anyway,' she said to herself as the hours passed and her hunger grew proportionally. 'If he doesn't come soon I'll die of hunger, and if he does, I'll have to listen to his superior, smug gloating and probably cook him dinner as well!'

Then, leaning out of the cupola window . . . 'Stupid

old bear, why don't you go someplace else to play? I'm not Goldilocks, you know. And this shouldn't be some kind of stupid game ... I'm getting awfully hungry. Please ... please go away!'

She kept it up, wavering dangerously between sadness and outright hysteria, until it was getting almost too dark to see the bear. Suddenly, without any warning, the animal loped out from behind the cabin, down the tower road and out of sight in the thick timber. Seana was amazed, incredulous. Then she, too, was in motion, scampering down the ladder and legging it for the cabin as quick as she could run.

Once inside, the shotgun in her shaking, tremulous hands, she stalked the windows like some defender of a pioneer fort, fearful of Indians. Then the reality struck her, and she raced to pour a tot of the medicinal brandy she kept for emergencies.

'Lord, I'm cracking up,' she gasped, the glass trembling in her fingers. 'Cabin fever, that's what it is. The whole wretched thing is just an hallucination!'

As the brandy fanned a gentle flame in her empty tummy, she almost managed to convince herself. A second glass, this one fuller than the first, and she was sneaking out the door, shotgun in hand (just in case) to make a cautious circuit of the porch.

'No bear,' she muttered to herself. 'No bear at all, never was a bear. Just my imagination. Couldn't be a bear anyway, bears don't play cat-and-mouse games with girls on forestry towers. But then what broke the string of cans on the porch, I wonder. And oh, my ... what left all these funny tracks in the mud, here? People tracks? Not with claws like that they're not!'

And she was scurrying back through the cabin door, shotgun held like a defiant banner. Once inside, she flung the bar over the door and rushed to close the flimsy curtains at the windows.

Shotgun lying across the table, she was half-way through cooking her dinner when the flame, without warning, died. 'Oh, no!' she cried angrily, vividly conscious of the fact that she couldn't possibly wrestle another hundred-pound propane bottle into position and keep an eye out for the bear at the same time.

'Resourcefulness, that's what I need,' she muttered aloud. 'That's what the pioneer women had, and whatever my grandmother could handle, I can do too. The heater . . . that's it! Lots of firewood right outside on the porch. I'll just finish cooking on the heater.'

No sooner said than done . . . after seven one-armed trips in which she toted firewood with one arm and kept the shotgun ready with the other. The result was total disarray of her neatly stacked firewood outside, and a worse mess inside.

But she had two days' supply of wood inside with her and the door was safely barred. Twenty minutes and another brandy later, the meal was finished and at least she wasn't starving any more . . . 'just mildly tiddly, that's all,' she giggled.

The gentle music of the heater had a soporific effect, soothing her both by warmth and by drowning out the myriad tiny sounds that she heard from the shadows outside. All were sounds she had long ago grown used to . . . a packrat bustling about on his evening rounds, squirrels having their bedtime scold, a bush rabbit chomping at the remains of the garden . . . but now each took on a threatening, ominous note.

Sipping at yet another brandy, Seana was almost comfortable cataloguing them in her mind, trying to convince herself she wasn't frightened and had no reason to be. Then a new sound intruded, and she shot bolt upright in her chair, grabbing in panic for the shotgun.

It was a deep, grunting squeal, an obscene sound

that combined with growlings and scuffling noises that seemed to come from right outside the door. It was the most horrible noise she had ever encountered, and there was only one possible explanation.

'The bear,' she muttered in a low whisper. 'It must be . . .'

During a brief lull in the racket, she waited for the sound of her warning system being disturbed, but it wasn't. Only the growling returned, this time off to the right of the doorway, but without tangible direction.

Seana rushed to the nearest window, but with more light now inside the cabin than out, she couldn't see a thing. 'Damn!' she cried, then rushed to close the grate on the heater and blew out her candles. She returned to the window to sit with her nose pressed flat against the glass, peering into the malignant darkness from where the grunting, growling noises continued.

She returned to huddle by the fire, but as the noises grew louder, more insistent, her fears grew more and more frantic. Finally she could take no more.

Quietly sneaking to the doorway, she quietly removed the bar, eased the door open—just two inches, no more—then stuck the muzzle of the shotgun through, pointed it carefully upward lest she shoot her Volkswagen, and pulled the trigger.

The blast lit up the night sky like a beacon, but Seana didn't see anything because she'd been holding the gun quite loosely and the recoil had thrown her back into the room with a badly bruised arm. But when the echoes had finished playing in the hills around her, she found that at least she'd stopped the growling sounds.

All was silent until the growing roar of a truck engine sounded and headlights threw eerie patterns into the sky as it rounded the final curve and shot into the clearing.

Ryan Stranger was on the ground and striding towards her before Seana could even think to put the shotgun away, and he quickly took it from her trembling fingers.

'If I'm not welcome, you only have to say so,' he said in his usual, sarcastic, bantering tone. 'There's no need to start shooting . . .' And then, marvellously, he stopped talking and just gathered her into his arms as she burst into tears and outright hysterics, sobbing and crying and ranting totally incomprehensible things about bears and noises and spooks in the night. He held her for what seemed like hours before gently easing her away from him and steering her into the cabin.

He closed the door, barred it at her insistence, then lit the candles and hauled out the coffee makings. And when Seana tried to speak, he shushed her.

'All in good time, ladybug,' he said. 'You sure do seem to have your troubles up here, and that's a fact.' Then he picked up the nearly empty brandy bottle and looked at her wearily. 'Humph . . . hitting the bottle too, I see. I think maybe you've been up here too long.'

The caustic comment did what nothing else might have accomplished in curing her fright. She felt the anger building inside her, and Ryan, too, seemed to notice it.

'Yeah, that's better,' he chuckled. 'You'll make more sense angry than hysterical. Now just settle down a minute and try telling me what *really* happened . . . okay?

'Why bother?' she snapped. 'All you'll do is tell me I did everything wrong anyway.'

He didn't dispute it. 'You sure as hell didn't stay in

the tower like you were told,' he retorted, and waved at the windows in an angry gesture. 'How much bloody protection do you think this place could offer?' he demanded. 'Any self-respecting bear could bust his way in here in thirty seconds flat.'

'Well, I was *hungry*,' she protested. 'And . . . and . . . oh, what's the use?'

'Well, just be glad he wasn't a damned sight hungrier,' Ryan scowled, rising to pour them each a cup of coffee. He handed Seana her cup, and although he shot her a withering glance when she deliberately added a shot of brandy, he didn't vocally object.

They sat, both of them silent, as they sipped at the scalding coffee, then Seana flinched violently as she heard once again the horrible sound outside.

Ryan leapt to his feet and extinguished the candles, then picked up the shotgun and eased his way to the door with Seana right at his heels.

'Will you get *back*!' he whispered, his voice a snarling hiss.

'No,' she replied just as adamantly. 'If you're going, I'm going too. You're not leaving me here alone.'

His reply was inaudible, a curt nod of his head against the starlight through the half-opened door. Outside, there was silence, then the shuffling, growling, *awful* noise began again. It was enough to set Seana's teeth on edge, and she felt herself trembling uncontrollably.

Ryan stood there, for ever, it seemed, listening intently. Then he turned and whispered cautiously, 'Have you got a flashlight?'

Seana spent some time finding it, then at his direction turned it on and off for a split second, just to be sure it worked.

'Right,' he said. 'Now I want you to stay right behind me, and I mean close. And be ready to switch it on the instant I tell you. Have you got that?'

He didn't wait for a reply, but began immediately stalking cautiously towards the sound. Seana reached out and grabbed at the back of his shirt, unable to see where they were going as she stumbled along with him, trying her best to move quietly. She still trembled with fear; or was it excitement? she wondered. Either way, she felt amazingly safe as she clung like a leech to his shadowy shape, treading almost on his heels as he padded down off the porch and eased his way around the edge of the cabin.

Ahead and slightly to the left, the grunting and growling took on a more immediate, more ominous note, and Ryan paused as if ready for action. Then he reached back and firmed Seana's grip on his shirt-tail before moving forward once more. As her eyes adjusted more to the indifferent light, Seana could now see how warily he held the shotgun, how carefully placed was each individual step that he took. And although she, too, was walking carefully, she often stumbled or stepped on a brittle, crackling twig.

Each time she did so, the sounds ahead would cease, and they would stand shock-still until the animal noises resumed. Then Ryan would move forward again, still with that intense caution.

They moved closer ... closer ... and finally she sensed his awareness of what lay before them. Halting, almost an animal himself with his head cast high and his nostrils sniffing at the faint breeze, he seemed to be looking upward, though Seana could see nothing and the snuffling, grotesque gruntings seemed to be all around them.

He reached back, took the hand holding the flashlight, and silently guided her until it was pointing where he wanted it. Then he lifted the shotgun to the ready and quietly said, 'Now!'

Seana snapped on the light, then stared, stricken, at the two tiny red eyes that peered myopically at them from head-high in a young jackpine not three feet away. One hand still clutching Ryan's shirt-tail, she could feel him holding back gulps of laughter as his body convulsed. The gun hung useless at his side, useless and unneeded.

The grunting, snuffling horror they had been tracking for what seemed like hours, the terror of the night which had driven Seana almost to hysterics, was only a porcupine!

As harmless an animal as could be, despite its porcine vocabulary—and Ryan knew it. Ryan had known all along, she suddenly realised as the laughter finally exploded from him.

CHAPTER SEVEN

SEANA was stunned. Then, as the realisation of his deliberate trickery grew, her anger grew with it, fomented by embarrassment and stricken pride.

And as if to add insult to injury, the porcupine took that instant to snuffle at her, quite clearly saying, 'Put out the light, lady.'

Turning from the poor harmless creature, she aimed the flashlight to where she could clearly see her way back to the cabin door, then she flashed it straight into Ryan's laughing eyes. Her own eyes were so blurred by tears and anger she could hardly see.

'You . . . you utter, contemptible swine!'

She spat out the words, then turned and stumbled away from him, oblivious of the lashing of unseen branches, of the still possible threat of the real bear, of everything but her own humiliation. When she reached the cabin, she paused only long enough to slam and bar the door and close every single curtain, then she blew out the candle again and flung herself on to her bed, the tears flowing in a sudden torrent.

She heard Ryan, a few minutes later, give one soft knock on the door, but she ignored him, her face buried in her pillow as she cried out every tension, every frustration of her entire summer. A moment later she heard his truck engine, but he didn't go far before it was switched off again.

Curious, she pulled back a corner of the curtain and peered out to find the truck parked at the far side of the clearing, a light now visible in the camper window. She deliberated momentarily whether to go and apologise, then let her stricken pride take charge and went back to bed instead.

'To hell with him,' she mumbled into the pillow. 'I hope the wretched bear comes back, Ryan Stranger, and eats your tyres for breakfast! And you with them . . . that'd take the smug grin off your stupid face!'

Then she wallowed into a fitful, restless slumber that ended seemingly minutes later with two loud bangs from the shotgun and the even louder, angry squeal of a very surprised bear. Seana came out of the bed in a rush, but in the ominous silence that followed she couldn't be sure if she dared go out to see what had happened. The light filtering in through the curtains belied the apparent brevity of her sleep, and she realised she was still wearing the clothes she had lain down in.

'Hey, ladybug . . . got the coffee on yet? Or are you still mad at me?' Ryan's voice held the normal traces of pure mockery, bringing back every vestige of Seana's anger from the evening before.

She flung open the door and stood there, staring angrily into eyes so green they seemed to sparkle at her. Green . . . and alive with hidden laughter. Devil!

'Of course I'm still angry,' she charged. 'What's the idea of shooting that stupid gun? Couldn't you get your friendly porcupine to squeal any other way?'

He stood there, silently regarding her with eyes that toured her slender figure from head to toe in a look that could have been a caress, but wasn't going to be allowed to be.

'I'd have thought you'd have him better trained than that,' she scorned, then slammed the door in his face and walked away. Ryan didn't take the hint, but opened the door and walked into the cabin with her.

'Porcupine, hell! That was a fat young grizzly bear, and tough enough to have caused you no end of problems. But he won't be back, I don't think, not after the surprise I just gave him. I found out why he likes you so much, too, but I don't suppose you're interested, so I'll go make my own coffee and won't bother showing you.'

Curiosity had defeated her before he was off the porch, and Seana trotted meekly after him, hating herself for being so easily manipulated. 'I'm probably not going to believe you, but show me anyway,' she said sulkily, and followed him as he walked around to the far back corner of the cabin, where a series of gouges had been slashed in the white clay surrounding the foundations.

'See there . . . that's where the rabbits have been at it, and our porcupine friend as well. It's a salt-lick, or at least a mineral deposit with something in it the animals need or like the taste of. See the bear claw marks? I sure hope he got enough, because I don't think he'll be back for a long time to come.'

'But what did you *do*?' Then she stopped, wide-eyed. 'You . . . you didn't . . .'

'I just gave him something else to think about,' Ryan said with a grin, then showed her the remaining shotgun shell and its load of coarse, chunky rock salt. 'I just let him get nicely into his digging, and when he turned his tail the right way I put some salt on it,' he laughed. 'By now he'll be five miles away and still running, looking for a puddle to sit in. But he'll remember where he got it, mark my words.'

Seana couldn't help but laugh at the mental picture of what must have happened, and at the identical advice she had been given over the radio the day before. Ryan waited patiently until she had finished, then said, 'Well, do I get my coffee now?'

She offered him breakfast as well, but only as a bribe to get him to shift the propane bottles for her. He managed that with maddening ease, then sat down to clean the shotgun and drink cup after cup of coffee while Seana managed to create the worst cooking performance of her life.

She was shamed almost beyond speech as she placed before him a plate of half-burned home-fried potatoes, soggy bacon and toast that was either too brown or not brown enough.

'I don't know what's the matter with me,' she said as he looked sceptically at the offering and then began to eat it as if it were perfect. 'I'm as nervous as a . . .'

'. . . new bride?' And he laughed out loud at the blush she couldn't prevent. 'Now, don't go getting mad all over again . . . it isn't your cooking that'll stop you snaring some poor, unsuspecting bachelor. What you're going to have to watch is that even disposition of yours.'

'Even? That's about the last thing I'd have expected anyone to say about my disposition,' she retorted.

'I think it's remarkably even,' he grinned. 'You're just mean all the time.' And he ducked as she made as if to throw the coffee pot at him. 'No, no more coffee, thanks. I've got a long walk ahead of me, and I don't want to be sloshing all the way,' he said. 'But I'll tell you what . . . there's a chunk of nice venison in the cooler in my truck. Why don't I bring you in half to practise on, and we'll have the rest for dinner when I get back. Unless of course you'd rather just leave the cooking to somebody who knows how.'

Seana bit her lip. Ryan couldn't keep on baiting her if she refused to play the game, didn't rise to the bait like a starving trout every time he offered it to her.

'I think that's a wonderful idea,' she replied with exaggerated sweetness. 'I've always believed in sexual equality, especially in the kitchen.'

'So do I,' he said, rising to his feet. 'In the kitchen.' And he halted long enough to plant an unexpected kiss on the tip of her nose before striding out on to the porch.

'Where are you going, anyway?' she asked, walking behind him as he strolled towards his truck. It was a reasonable enough question, but the look he suddenly gave her made it sound horribly wifely. She regretted asking it as soon as the words were out.

'Oh, back over west there a bit,' he replied casually. 'I want to take a little check on that white moose of mine before some city hunter beats me to it.'

'The moose? You can't shoot that moose. You just can't!' Seana's protest kicked her voice up to almost an hysterical pitch, but Ryan either didn't notice or didn't care.

'Ladybug, I can do just about anything that I want to do, except maybe spend five whole minutes with you that doesn't end up in a slanging match,' he replied, the smile replaced by what might almost have been a sort of grim sadness.

'Now I'm going to spend the rest of this day walking through alder thickets and mud and brush and God knows what else. And when I find that moose—and I will—if I decide to shoot it there is not one thing that you or anybody else can do about it. Now is that clear enough for you?'

He turned away and stepped lightly up into his camper, emerging a moment later with a huge, paper-wrapped parcel which he handed over as if expecting her to refuse. 'Here's our dinner, which will be a lot easier to cook if it's thawed first,' he said. 'Do you suppose you can manage that?'

'I'm sure there'll be something in one of my many cook books that will explain in simple terms how to thaw out a piece of meat,' she retorted angrily, her own temper flaring to match his own.

'Good,' he replied hotly, and turned away to collect

his rifle and pack, then stride away down the trail towards the spring without another word.

'But you let me tell you something, Ryan Stranger,' she shouted after him. 'If you shoot my moose, you'll get your venison with arsenic in it! Do you hear me?'

If he did hear, he gave no indication, and within a minute he was out of sight. Seana slammed back into the cabin, did the breakfast dishes just in time to catch the morning schedule, then climbed up the tower to resume her duties. For once there wasn't a trace of smoke to be seen, which left her free to use her vantage point and powerful binoculars to monitor Ryan's progress far below.

It was fascinating to watch; he moved through the dense undergrowth with deceptive speed, but the most surprising thing was how directly he aimed for the very area where she would have expected to find the moose herself, though she couldn't find the animal in the glasses.

He knows. He knows exactly where he's going, she thought. But he couldn't. He hasn't been on the tower all summer. He hasn't been up here for weeks. How can he be that sure?

Just how sure Ryan was became evident within half an hour when the ghostly shape of the moose suddenly reared up from behind a deadfall where he had been lying in the shade. Seana's viewpoint revealed that Ryan was within a quarter of a mile of the beast, although she couldn't tell if he could see it or not. The way he was going, however, he would practically stumble over the animal, and as she watched, Seana began talking to herself—and to the distant pair—without being totally aware she was doing it.

'Oh, get away from there, you stupid beast!' she cried. 'How can you be so vulnerable? Oh, Ryan Stranger, I hate you! I really do. If you shoot that moose I think I really *will* poison your food, and it would serve you right!'

She was so angry that she contemplated going down for the shotgun in hopes that she might be able to startle the animal, but then reason prevailed as she lowered the glasses and realised just how far from her the moose and Ryan really were.

All she could do was watch helplessly as the man slowly made his way closer and closer to where the unsuspecting animal stood calmly browsing. She was concentrating so hard on that, she didn't even notice the arrival of the truck in the clearing below or the first time Ralph Beatty shouted up to her.

When she did hear him, however, she leaned half out the open window and called frantically to him to come and join her. But by the time Ralph had reached the cupola, which suddenly shrank in size as his bulk filled it, both Ryan and the moose had moved out of sight.

'Oh . . . damn!' Seana exclaimed.

'That's not much of a welcome,' Ralph grinned. 'What's the matter, Seana, are you fighting with Ryan again? I see his truck's here, so I suppose he's off chasing his moose.'

'He is, and I think it's just rotten,' she exclaimed angrily. 'Isn't there anything you can do to stop him, Ralph? If he shoots that moose, I . . . I don't know what I'll do, but he'll regret it, you can be sure of that!'

'What are you talking about? Ryan's not going to shoot that moose,' he said, only to be interrupted as Seana attempted to shout him down.

'He is! He told me so, for goodness' sake!'

Ralph looked at her, a surprised, confused look that made him shake his head wonderingly.

'I think you've been out here alone too long, dear

girl. The absolute last thing Ryan would do is shoot that moose. I tell you that, and it's true. Although,' he mused, 'I wouldn't put it past him to shoot *at* it.'

'I . . . I don't understand,' Seana replied, her eyes still hot with anger. 'You're not making any sense at all. I tell you he's going to shoot it. My moose . . . my white moose. He is! He told me so.'

Ralph ignored her then, and stepped over to pick up the binoculars so that he could scan the area. 'Where is he?' he asked wearily, and carefully followed Seana's directions. 'Ah, there they are,' he mused at something Seana couldn't see. 'God, what a beautiful beast, and what a magnificent set of antlers!'

'Will you stop talking about it and do something?' she screamed, grabbing the binoculars away from him so that she, too, could see what was happening.

Ralph relinquished them without an argument, then settled himself in Seana's chair at the chart table and waited patiently as she muttered and scowled and heaped curses on the head of the unheeding Ryan.

'Now listen,' he said then, 'did Ryan actually tell you he was going out to *shoot* that moose?'

'Well, of course he did,' she raged. 'And when I tried to talk him out of it he got really mad . . . said it was *his* moose and he'd shoot it if he damned well pleased. The rotten devil!'

Ralph's booming laughter rumbled through the confined space like thunder as he doubled up and howled with uncontrolled mirth. Seana didn't think it one bit funny, but her protests were useless until the laughter had run its course.

'Oh, dear,' Ralph sighed. 'You and Ryan really do *work* at not getting along, don't you? I mean, really work at it. Don't you ever see when he's leading you down the garden path, Seana? Hell, all Ryan has to do is look at you and you get so riled up you believe any damned thing he says and put the worst possible interpretation on it to boot.'

'That's ridiculous!' But it was true and she knew it; her comment was only a futile attempt to cover up her own confusion. Had Ryan done it to her *again*?

'I'd have thought he'd have told you about that moose by now,' said Ralph, blithely ignoring her comment. 'But you were probably too busy fighting with him to give him a chance. It really is *his* moose, in a way. He rescued it when a poacher shot its mother about five years ago, and he hand-raised it until it was old enough to look after itself—not the best of naturalist practices, but understandable because of the rare colour. Anyway, he ended up bringing it out here and releasing it in the wildest, least accessible country he could find.

'I think he once told me it took him two days just to get there by horse, with the moose calf following him. And four days to get out again, because the damned thing kept trying to stay with him, of course.

'At least twice a year, ever since then, he's taken time near the start of hunting season to locate the animal and try to steer it back into the rough country, where nobody's likely to find it. Up until this year it's been pretty easy, but now that it's been sighted I don't much like the poor moose's chances. Unless, of course, he can spook it into some *really* bad country where even skidoos can't get once the snow comes. I personally think he's dreaming, but knowing Ryan I also know he has to try.'

The explanation was simple, so simple. But Seana's reaction was a complicated and contradictory muddle of irate, hurt feelings and injured pride.

'That rotten, dirty so-and-so!' she cried. 'He did that deliberately, that's what. Deliberately! He as much as told me he was going to shoot that moose. Well, I'll show Mr Ryan Stranger a trick or two before I'm done, you just wait and see! I'll make him wish he'd never so much as mentioned moose to me!'

Ralph laughed, then got up and opened the hatch. 'Have fun,' he said. 'And I'm sure you will, knowing the way the two of you carry on. But some of us, unfortunately, have to work for a living. And since I'm one of them, I'd best be on my way.'

'Why don't you try and get back for supper?' Seana asked, blurting out the invitation as quickly as it occurred to her. 'I've got some really lovely venison and I'd love to have you share it.'

'Okay . . . see you about eight o'clock, if that isn't too late,' Ralph agreed, and if he suspected her intentions, he didn't show it.

The rest of the day, fortunately, was quite peaceful. Seana spent most of it trying to locate Ryan and *his* moose, but they seemed to have moved down behind a ridge that obscured her view.

She wasn't quite sure how she would handle Ryan if he returned before Ralph showed up, but she became increasingly determined as the day wore on to do something to even the score. The humiliation of being taken in yet again by his cunning made any thought of revenge especially sweet.

Ralph got back exactly at the time he had promised, and apart from showing mild surprise that Ryan wasn't back yet, he said nothing about his friend, apparently thinking it of no really great significance that Ryan was roaming around somewhere out there with night only minutes away.

Seana, mindful of Mrs Jorgensen's instructions about wild meat, soon had the venison sliced into enormous steaks that sizzled enticingly in the heavy cast-iron frying pan. They were just settling down to eat when a voice from the open doorway caused Seana to pause, fork halfway to her mouth and an unexpected flush of surprise rising along her throat.

'My, my . . . isn't this a fine example of gratitude! I bring the woman fresh meat and as soon as my back is turned she feeds it to somebody else. How are you, Ralph? Getting enough to eat? You're a braver man than I am, my friend . . . there's probably enough arsenic in that steak to kill a grizzly bear . . . or were you saving the poisoned bit for me, ladybug?'

'She must be saving it for you,' Ralph muttered around a mouthful of tender steak. 'Mine's just fine, thanks.'

'So it should be, considering the trouble I went to getting it,' Ryan replied. 'Ah, well, I suppose I can make do with a can of beans, although it really is stretching friendship a bit far . . .'

'Oh, stop it!' Seana snorted. 'There's more than enough for you and you know it. In fact, why don't you start on this,'—pointing to her own plate—'while I get busy cooking some more?'

'I wouldn't dream of it,' Ryan replied. 'Take the food right out of your mouth? No, I've got to get cleaned up anyway, so you go ahead and enjoy your meal.'

'Why must you always go out of your way to be difficult?' Seana snapped, and while Ryan merely looked at her innocently, Ralph chuckled around yet another mouthful of steak and then joined in the conversation.

'My, but you two get along beautifully,' he laughed. 'I really think you ought to get married; it's a shame to spoil two houses with you.'

Seana gasped at the remark, but Ryan gave her no chance to answer.

'Not likely. It'd be like sleeping with a rattlesnake,' he replied. 'You'd never know which night would be your last. If anybody's going to marry Seana, I think it should be you, Ralph. You've got a nice steady job and money in the bank. And at least *you* can talk to her without starting a war every time you open your mouth.'

He looked at Seana, his eyes roving over her slender body as if she were on an auction block. The expression in his eyes was unreadable, not the usual mocking light, but not anything else she could interpret, either.

'No . . . not for me,' he said then. 'Give me a nice quiet farm girl who knows how to cook, clean and keep the bed warm without hostility. I'd starve to death in a week on the diet of hot tongue and cold shoulder that Seana dishes up.'

'Oh, I don't know,' Ralph replied, speaking as if Seana weren't even *there*! 'This venison was sure good; I think she can cook fairly well when she puts her mind to it. The problem is that whenever you're around she can't keep her mind on what she's doing.'

'She's too busy thinking of nasty remarks,' Ryan added. 'You'd really think she could be nice *once* in a while, but then maybe she really wants to be an old maid. I'll bet that's it . . . she doesn't want to get married at all. She'd rather burn her bra and run around screaming about sexual equality.'

'I can't imagine that,' said Ralph. 'Why should a woman want equality? They've already got most of the advantages as it is. If anybody should be demanding equality, it's us!' And he glanced slyly to where Seana was quietly fuming, her meal forgotten.

'If you think you're going to get my goat, you're both sadly mistaken,' she replied with as calm a voice as she could muster. 'And just for the record, I wouldn't marry either one of you on a bet! You,' she said to Ralph, 'eat too much. And you,' to Ryan, 'talk too much. Now go and get cleaned up and your steak will be ready when you are.'

Ralph laughed. 'She's learning,' he said, again treating Seana as if she were absent.

'Um ... slowly, though,' Ryan replied, then ducked out the door when Seana flung a fork at him in a deliberate gesture of mock rage.

Ralph was done with his meal and ready to go back on patrol when Ryan returned to the cabin, changed into clean clothes and with water still hanging in droplets from the tips of his beard. 'I'd like to stay, but duty calls,' the wildlife officer said. 'That's the worst part of this job; I always have to go to work just when the party's getting interesting.'

They made their farewells, then Ryan sat down to his dinner while Seana bustled about making fresh coffee and trying to avoid his deliberate, sensuous appraisal of her movements. He ate in silence, then abruptly asked, 'What are your plans when the season's over?'

'I ... I'm not sure yet. Why?' she replied, deliberately not mentioning Mrs Jorgensen's proposal and her own acceptance of it.

'Do you want to stay up here, or do you miss the city so much you'll be going straight back?'

'To the city? Not if I can help it,' she replied, honest in that much, at least.

He looked slightly surprised at that, then frowned and returned to his interrogation. 'But you haven't got a job lined up yet ... or anything?'

He was obviously leading up to something, but for the life of her she couldn't imagine what. 'Well, I've had an offer or two,' she lied. 'Old Mike over at Saddle Hills wants me to spend the winter teaching him to bake bread, and ...'

'Damn it, be serious!' he snapped in an unexpected

show of temper that immediately sparked Seana's own.

'Well, I might, if you'd stop beating around the bush,' she retorted. 'Why can't you just come out and say what you mean, for a change?'

All right . . . I might have something you'd be interested in. How's that?' he growled.

'You? *You?* What kind of job could you possibly have for me?' she jeered. 'According to you I'm a walking disaster area, remember? Unsafe to be left alone, incompetent, useless . . .'

Hands like steel claws reached out to take Seana's shoulders, and for several seconds she was picked up and shaken like a naughty child. 'Damn it! Can't we talk about anything without you starting a fight?' he demanded. 'Now sit down and shut up and listen, or I'll have you over my knee next!'

She was so surprised at the physical threat that she did as he ordered, eyes wide with astonishment. He was really angry! But why? she wondered.

'What kind of a typist are you?' he asked after sliding back into his own chair. 'Not necessarily fast, but can you type nice tidy, clean, accurate copy?'

'Yes.'

'Good,' he said. 'That's settled, then.'

'What's settled? What are you talking about?' she demanded, forgetting her resolve to be quiet.

'Well, when you get done up here you can spend a few months typing this damned textbook I'm working on,' he said. 'There's three hundred and fifty pages, so far, and it's in pretty rough shape, but with your zoological training you should have no trouble. Couldn't do any worse than the typist who did the last one. She didn't know anything about the subject and she made some awful mistakes—gave the proof-readers a helluva time, and me with them. The publisher wasn't much impressed either.'

He paused and looked enquiringly at Seana. 'What are you staring at? Have I just grown two heads or something?'

He was closer than he dreamed. A sudden flash of insight had struck Seana with the force of a thunderbolt, and she was wondering how she could have been so long putting two and two together.

'You're ... you're R. G. Stranger!' The words emerged in a fog of total astonishment, and some of the confusion seemed to spill across the table.

'Isn't that allowed?' he asked, a wondering look on his face.

He might have saved his breath. '*You're* the R. G. Stranger who did the master's thesis on the relationships between wetland habitat and moose populations? And the later study into the effects of oil exploration and access on moose in the Whitecourt forest? I ... I just don't believe it!' Seana cried.

'Oh, you don't?' Sarcasm crept into his voice as he stared back at her. 'What did you expect, white hair and Coke-bottle glasses? It isn't necessary to be a centenarian to be a researcher, or hadn't you noticed?'

'Oh, it's got nothing to do with your age,' Seana blurted, then halted in embarrassed confusion. But Ryan finished what she was fumbling to get out without being insulting, and he was much more brutal about it.

'But you thought I was just a poor ignorant backwoods boy, is that it?' he said with a wry twist to his generous mouth. 'No manners, no style, no education ... just a rough, crude country hick.' And his voice became increasingly caustic as he went on. 'Well, let me suggest, Miss Muldoon, that you are the worst person I have ever seen for making assumptions based on things you know nothing about. Now do you want the typing job or not?'

'Well . . . yes,' she said, 'but I . . . I can't take it.'

'Why not? Or is it the fact that you'd be staying under my roof that bothers you? Well, it shouldn't, because while you might be there, I won't. I've got a full guiding schedule for the rest of the season and I'll be too far away to come home at weekends, just to be bitched at.'

'You're a fine one to be complaining about people making assumptions,' she snapped, over-defensive and not caring if he realised it or not. Then she outlined Mrs Jorgensen's offer and found to her astonishment that he immediately agreed with her acceptance of it.

'It solves a lot of problems on both sides,' he said. 'And don't worry about Hutton; I just happen to know he's quite impressed with the way you've handled things up here. He's a good man, even if he won't listen to me.'

'It doesn't solve your problem, though, does it?' Seana asked, deliberately ignoring his attempt to bait her. 'And actually, I would like to do that typing for you, if you still want me to. I . . . was quite impressed with your work when I was at university.'

'Well, thanks . . . for both the compliment and the offer,' he smiled. 'And now I'd better be going . . . wouldn't want to compromise your reputation any more than I already have.'

Seana walked with him to his truck, suddenly, surprisingly at ease, yet still with one question she just had to ask.

'Why didn't you tell me the truth about the white moose in the first place?' She asked it very gently, without any hint of sarcasm. 'You were deliberately trying to get my goat, but why bother?'

The reply was anything but what she might have expected. Wordlessly, Ryan turned and pulled her against him, seeking her lips and finding them with unerring skill.

Seana responded without thinking, her body going with the pressure of his arms, her own arms lifting to clasp around his neck and her response heightening with his as the kiss continued. His hands moved along her back, stirring her passion as his kisses rained on her lips, then his fingers shifted subtly lower, caressing her hips, pulling her against the hardness of his body.

She could feel the wiry tickle of his beard on her cheeks, then along her throat as his lips moved down into the opening of her shirt while his hands continued their gentle exploration of her body.

Her own passion rose to meet his, her hands moving like creatures separate from the rest of her as they stroked at the nape of his neck, explored the hard muscles of his shoulders and back, then crept between them to seek the furry warmth of his chest.

His lips traced a delicate pattern across the top of her bosom, then up her throat to where his teeth could nibble at the lobe of her ear.

'Why bother?' he whispered. 'This is why.' And his fingers expertly slipped the buttons of her blouse, then ran like fire over her exposed breasts, firming them, turning their peaks to such tenderness Seana could have screamed with delight at his touch.

His lips followed his fingers, the coolness of his mouth merely adding to her pleasure, floating her further and further from all reason.

'Ryan . . .' She whispered his name even as he pulled her closer, forcing their bodies together so that her breasts were crushed against the hardness of his chest, her hips writhing against his. But she wasn't close enough; she wanted to be part of him, united with him in a single entity that would merge their passions into one all-consuming flame.

'Not now.' Had she said that? She had not! But even as she wondered, Ryan's arms tensed, forcing her just far enough away from him to break the spell. 'Not now,' he said again, and then he was kissing her again, only this time it was a kiss of pure passion, without tenderness, without consideration. For an instant she accepted it, but then she recoiled, unsure of herself, and he let her—helped her—go.

'Some day, maybe,' he said, 'when you're older.'

There was a thin-veiled innuendo there, enough to make Seana jerk back with anger at the tone in his voice, the guarded, deliberate look in his eyes. But she said nothing, merely stared at him, trying to figure out what had changed him, what had taken the colour from their lovemaking.

'You're a lot easier to resist when you're angry,' he told her, leaning down to kiss her lightly on the forehead. As he stepped back, she saw the impish gleam in his eyes. 'And besides, it's so easy to make you angry.'

The proof was how long she stood, fuming, after he had got into his truck and driven away down the mountain.

And it *was* easy to get her goat, Seana decided as she lay sleepless in her bunk several hours later. Easy, because she made it easy, because she kept opening her mouth and shoving in her feet, but mostly because she loved Ryan Stranger so much she was totally vulnerable to his every mood, his every word.

'And that,' she said aloud, 'has got to stop.'

She spent the rest of the week deliberately considering all her past encounters with Ryan, especially her own reactions to his blatant baiting and prodding.

And on Saturday, Mrs Jorgensen arrived for a visit with yet another example of Ryan's own peculiar logic. In addition to her usual complement of baked goods, the white-haired woman unloaded two stout cardboard boxes, each of them stuffed to the brim with papers and photos and scribbled notes.

And a letter: 'I thought you might like to have a look at what you're getting yourself into if you decide to take on the typing job,' it said. 'I think your tower job is almost over; you'll have snow there within three weeks. Please keep an eye on *our* moose and I'll do the same for *your* goat, which I still have, I'm sure.'

He hadn't bothered to sign it, but there was no doubt of the sender. Well aware of Mrs Jorgensen's interest, Seana handed her the note with the casual comment, 'He writes a fairly nice hand, doesn't he?'

'Oh, definitely,' her friend agreed. 'But what I want to know is when's the wedding? Or do you have to wait until you get your goat back?'

'There isn't going to be any wedding,' Seana objected. 'That's just his weird sense of humour.'

'Oh yeah? Then why is your face so red?'

'Sunburn,' Seana shrugged, deliberately being as casual about the whole issue as she could be.

'At this time of year? Oh, come now. I may be old but I'm not stupid. And what's wrong with admitting you're attracted to Ryan? He's handsome, a good hard worker . . . most girls around here would think of him as a good catch.'

'Which only shows that *most* girls don't know him very well at all,' Seana retorted. 'He's handsome, I'll give you that. But he's also egotistical, chauvinistic, overbearing, arrogant and generally obnoxious.'

'You forgot rough, tough and nasty, big, bad, bold and expensive,' Mrs Jorgensen snorted. 'What's the matter . . . are you two feuding again?'

'Not that I know of. He'd hardly send all this to anybody he was feuding with, would be?'

Mrs Jorgensen wasn't swayed by that argument. 'I know very well why he sent it,' she said. 'The same

reason he's spent more time up here this summer than
he has in the last five years. Don't be fooled by ap-
pearances, dear. All this . . . typing . . . is just his way
of keeping you handy so he'll be able to do some serious
courting once the guiding season's over. And don't say
you hadn't thought of that yourself, although you
might be best not to admit it when he's within hearing.'

'I . . . he . . . he wouldn't,' Seana protested, flustered
because she genuinely hadn't thought of it. But I will,
she thought, and wondered if she really dared hope
that Mrs Jorgensen was right.

'What? No suspicions at all? And you have the nerve
to deny you're in love with the man! Oh, Seana,' Mrs
Jorgensen sighed, 'I'd think about it if I were you.
You may not *want* to be in love with Ryan, but I think
you certainly are. And best you admit it, to yourself if
nobody else.'

No sarcasm there, just a kind, genuine concern
against which Seana had no defences.

'But he doesn't even like me,' she protested. 'All we
ever do is fight . . . every single time we meet. As soon
as either one of us opens their mouth, there's a war
going on.'

'So what? You're communicating, aren't you? Or are
you going to tell me you're just dog-and-catting it
without any feelings at all?'

'Oh, there are feelings all right. I make him angry
and he makes me angry. He told Ralph—right in front
of me—that he just wants a quiet farm girl who'll cook,
clean and keep the bed warm. But he never even gives
me a chance. He just goes out of his way to get my
goat, and of course I let him . . . I think I even help
him!'

Mrs Jorgensen laughed. 'A quiet farm girl? That,
my dear, is a great load of something else from the

farm—and that I guarantee.' And she laughed again.
'What's more, if you believe it you're even more gullible than I think. Don't you imagine Ryan's had more
than his share of chances with nice, quiet farm girls?
Bored stupid in two days, that's what he'd be. At least
you know you're not boring him, or he wouldn't keep
coming back for more.'

'I don't know if I'm boring him or not, but I do
know I'm stupid to care,' Seana retorted. 'And as for
gullible—well, I think perhaps I'm too gullible to be
involved with Ryan or any other man. Maybe I should
just give it all away and go back to Edmonton as soon
as the first snow comes.'

She could feel the tears puddling behind her eyes,
but she no longer cared whether or not her feelings
were hidden. 'Look at me,' she cried. 'I'm nothing but
a bundle of nerves. I'm either high as a kite or down in
the dumps so far it's frightening. And all because of
Ryan Stranger? Oh, I need my head examined, that's
what I need!'

'What you need is the end of the fire season and a
chance to sort yourself out under circumstances that
are a little closer to normal,' Mrs Jorgensen replied. 'I
think you've coped marvellously up here, Seana, and
so does Ryan, no matter what he tells *you*. But it's not
a normal existence, there's no stability, no . . . no roots.
If I were you I'd just let the whole matter drop until
you're back in Grande Prairie, or Edmonton if you
absolutely must. There's only a few weeks to go up
here anyway.'

CHAPTER EIGHT

THE snow came even sooner than Ryan had predicted. It was an inch deep on the ground around the cabin exactly two weeks after the date on his brief letter.

For Seana, those two weeks were a time of intense debate between her emotions and her intellect, with no real clear-cut winner. The entire debate was hampered by her growing involvement with Ryan's first-draft manuscript, which she was slowly but surely getting into some vague form of organisation.

He was, she had to agree, no typist. And there was definitely far more to organising a textbook than she'd ever imagined. But it was fascinating work, and she fairly itched to have a typewriter there in the tower with her so that she could really begin.

She had already sorted out the masses of notes and diagrams and photographs into what she was fairly certain would be the proper order. And she had made considerable notes to herself to cover the required footnotes and captions. All that remained now was the final assembly and the typing itself.

Looking from her tower across a landscape no longer familiar because of its faint shroud of snow, she slammed down the papers she had been sorting and shook her head angrily. It was no longer possible to deny that the end of her season was almost at hand, and for some reason it bothered her.

Too, she was lonely. The press of work had kept Mrs Jorgensen from a planned visit; Ralph was busy chasing poachers far to the south, and Ryan Stranger was . . . wherever Ryan was. Nobody Seana had been in radio contact with had run across him, or at least his name hadn't come up during either the regular schedules or the increasingly irregular gossip sessions that heralded the closing of the fire season.

Increasing snows had already closed several of the higher mountain towers in the southern parts of the district where the Rocky Mountains angled eastward to form the Alberta-British Columbia boundary. And each tower closed meant one less familiar voice on the radio network, one less voice that belonged to someone Seana felt she knew despite never having actually seen them.

She had come awake that morning as if her body had already known about the overnight snowfall; she had begun the day with a joyous shout of welcome to the snow. But the morning schedule announced that there had been no snow at either Saddle Hills or Codesa tower, and her own white blanket of happiness disappeared well before noon. Even old Mike's prediction of more snow to come couldn't brighten a day that had suddenly gone ragged round the edges.

'There'll be more tonight,' he said. 'And probably a heavy fall the next night. I bake bread tomorrow, and I think it's the last I'll bake in this tower this year.'

But he was wrong. There wasn't even a good, solid frost that night, and Seana spent the next day, too, in a fit of blues and uncertainty. She tried hard to fight it off, using an arduous spell of woodchopping and a long session of sewing by lamplight, but when she tucked into her bunk that night it was to toss and turn through hours of nightmares and tormented dreams.

And still no snow the next day, though the skies were leaden with ominous clouds. Seana climbed the tower as if she was a hundred years old, hating every single step and cursing the chill from the iron rungs of the ladder. Once at the top, she almost turned round and climbed back down with hardly a look. There was nothing to see anyway; all around her, the cloud hung like a soggy blanket. And it was cold ... far colder than at ground level.

Shivering, she waited for the morning sked, squealing with delight when the towerman from Codesa reported snow. Then Mike came on to report that it was also starting to snow at Saddle Hills tower, and as Seana's turn came she saw the first, flickering white flakes drifting down outside her windows.

The radios fairly crackled with excitement as all three shouted their news, then a new voice came on the air to put a damper on their enthusiasm.

It was Frank Hutton, ominous only because he hadn't been expected and more than welcome once he had announced his news.

He wasted few words, simply informed each in their turn that the season was officially over. Only for Seana did he have any special message, and this, too, was short and to the point.

'Please see me in my office first thing Monday morning, Miss Muldoon.' And that was it! For Seana it meant the end of her exile, the start of a whole new life. And yet, during the three days she spent packing, stacking up the remaining firewood, putting away the instruments and closing down the tower and cabin for the winter, it was also a time of melancholy.

Would she ever come back to this place, she wondered, and indeed would she even want to? It had been her home, but unless it was she who took White Mountain Tower again next year, it would be somebody else's home then. And, somehow, she knew that she wouldn't be back, not permanently.

But that wasn't the issue when she faced Frank Hutton in his office, as ordered, on the Monday morning. He had much more immediate issues to discuss, and lost no time doing so.

'When was it you planned to leave, Mrs Jorgensen?' he barked into the intercom before Seana had even sat down.

'Two weeks yesterday,' came the reply from the outer office. 'That's November the fifth.'

Frank Hutton raised his eyes to meat Seana's. 'And would that suit you, Miss Muldoon?'

'Oh, yes, that would be just fine,' she replied, a trifle nervous because of his gruffness. There hadn't been so much as a word of welcome, much less any comment on her summer's work, and Seana was beginning to wonder.

'Good. You did a fine job at White Mountain Tower; if you can handle Mrs Jorgensen's job nearly as well there'll be no problems at all.' The compliment was couched in his usual gruff tones and clearly indicated that the conversation was over. Seana rose and walked towards the door, wondering if she should say thank you or just be grateful for small mercies and get out while she could.

She was turning the doorknob when he spoke again, unexpectedly and into the intercom rather than to Seana herself. 'Mrs Jorgensen! Please have the records show that Miss Muldoon ended her tower season officially on November . . . third.'

Seana turned in surprise, astounded at the generosity, but she was halted immediately by a careless wave of dismissal and a slow, deliberate wink. She could only smile her thanks and then, in a spirit of elation at the fortnight's paid holiday, follow it with a brisk, snappy salute. And as she passed through the door she could almost have sworn that she actually saw Frank Hutton smile.

'It must have been a trick of the light,' Mrs

Jorgensen insisted when they met later that morning for coffee. 'He wouldn't dare risk his reputation so blatantly.' Then she laughed. 'Don't worry about a thing,' she said. 'You'll have no problems with Frank Hutton. He comes across like a bear with a sore tooth, but underneath it all he's soft as butter, although he doesn't yet realise that anybody's noticed. Just don't let him get your goat, that's all.'

Seana fancied she saw one white eyebrow twitch slightly at the mention of her infamous *goat*, and she was reminded of her friend's comments during Mrs Jorgensen's last visit to the tower.

'Oh, I'm sure there won't be any problems,' she replied, deciding to ignore the jibe if that was what it had been. 'And it's only for a few months, after all. I'm sure we can keep from each other's throats for that long.'

'A *few* months? It'll be six months, if I have anything to say about it . . . so long as there's snow on the ground here and providing of course that the money holds out. And I'm not trading one winter for another, either. I'll stay in Scandinavia only long enough to see if I've any relatives who either remember me or care . . . then it's sunny Spain or the Greek islands. Who knows, maybe I'll find myself a rich continental boy-friend and stay even longer.'

Seana laughed aloud at the suggestion. Since her return to Grande Prairie, she found it increasingly difficult to imagine why she'd ever worried about falling in with her friend's plans. Everything was coming together just as if it had been planned long in advance.

Up to, and including, she found, Ryan's conviction that she would be doing his typing for him. She had arrived at Mrs Jorgensen's to find a rented electric typewriter and several reams of quality bond already waiting for her, along with the usual brief, to-the-point Ryan Stranger note.

'Three carbons; footnotes in script; captions all in CAPITAL LETTERS, please. See you for Hallowe'en, maybe. Don't turn into a pumpkin . . . or a witch! p.s. The goat is thriving.'

Which should have made her furious, but didn't. Instead of her usual fiery temper at Ryan's baiting, she felt only a soft, warming glow. Then she chided herself sternly with a warning not to start trying to read things into the note that mightn't be there at all.

One major bonus, depending on the viewpoint, of her summer in the tower had been a trimming of every excess inch from an already tidy figure, and Seana soon discovered that she would need most of her holiday pay just to renew her wardrobe. She had had to spend an hour with needle and thread just to provide herself with a walking-around dress to do her shopping in, she had lost so much weight on her rigorous summer job.

And with two weeks to do it in, she was almost disappointed to find that she really needed only a single day to find the clothes she wanted. One evening after dinner she treated Mrs Jorgensen to an impromptu fashion parade of all her purchases.

First, the work clothes. A selection of jersey dresses, mostly in simple styles and with a minimum of frills. Also, three smartly-tailored pant suits, one in a rich caramel colour, one in dusky rose and the third in a deep hunting green. And two pairs of boots to complement the various outfits.

But the highlight of the day's shopping was a long, clinging evening gown in a shade of violet that perfectly matched the colour of Seana's eyes. On sale. Half price. And too expensive even at that, but she just hadn't been able to resist.

'And I don't blame you; it's perfect,' raved Mrs Jorgensen. 'And who cares about the price if you can get that effect? What's more, I've got a shawl that will be perfect with it; I'll just go and get it.'

She was away somewhere at the back of the house, therefore, when the doorbell rang, leaving Seana to answer it. She felt a bit silly in the sleeveless, backless and—she feared—too low-cut dress as she shyly opened the door to receive a piercing wolf-whistle from the tall young man who stood there with snow frosting the fur on his hat and the ruff of his blue service parka.

'If I'd known this was on, I'd have come earlier,' Ralph said admiringly. 'Very, very nice . . . and just for me?'

'Of course not, silly. Come in before I freeze to death,' she replied, stepping back from the biting wind in the doorway.

They arrived in the living room just as Mrs Jorgensen returned with the shawl she had been seeking, and Seana was immediately cajoled into finishing her modelling role despite the additional observer. Then, fortunately, she fled to her room to change back into jeans and a sweatshirt before joining Ralph and Mrs Jorgensen for coffee.

Ralph wasted little time before announcing what he had come for; he wanted Seana to accompany him to the city's most prestigious Hallowe'en party. 'All I'm sorry about is that it's a masquerade affair, which might make it a bit tricky to wear that dress,' he said.

But even the compliment didn't make the decision any easier. She had Ryan's note, but even taking it at its best, he only said *maybe* he would see her at Hallowe'en. Only four days to go, and there had been no word at all, so should she reject the offer of a dear friend and find herself at home, waiting for a man who might not even show up?

No, she decided. That would be playing into Ryan's hands just a bit too easily, not to mention dangerously. Maybe it was time he learned that modern girls didn't sit waiting until the last minute for the sake of gratifying the male ego.

'I'd love to go,' she said, blatantly ignoring the look from Mrs Jorgensen that told her she wasn't fooling her friend one bit.

'You're playing a dangerous game,' Mrs J. told her after Ralph had left. 'Be careful you don't get burned, playing with fire like that.'

'I am *not* playing with fire,' Seana replied stoutly. 'I just have the feeling that I'm being taken far too much for granted, and I mean to put a stop to it.'

She smiled then, as much to herself as to placate Mrs Jorgensen. 'It's too bad that dress isn't black; it would make a splendid witch's outfit, don't you think?'

'I think it would be bewitching, to say the least,' her friend replied, 'but I'd watch it if I were you. Your spells might start to backfire on you. I don't need any crystal ball to see what witchery you're planning, Seana Muldoon, and I think you'd be wiser to start planning a wedding gown.'

With that, she stalked away to bed, leaving Seana to sit pensively alone, plotting and scheming her plans for the Hallowe'en party and wondering whether Ryan would even be there. In her own room, later, Seana admired the mauve dress again before retiring, and when she finally slept it was to dream of it, only in the dream it was white. Then the dream slid into a nightmare as she realised that the man beside her was faceless, and the eyes that gleamed from the void were a wicked, piercing, devilish green.

She woke up in tears, her body drenched with perspiration, and had great difficulty getting back to sleep. But in the morning she was more convinced than ever about what she would wear to the masquerade ball.

It took her right until the last minute to prepare for the party, but the result, she thought, was well worth it. Provided, of course, the elusive Ryan bothered to show.

She had still heard nothing from him by the afternoon of Hallowe'en, a circumstance which more than justified, in her own mind, the decision to go to the party with Ralph. And as darkness fell on the eve of ghouls and goblins, bringing with it a growing number of diminutive spooks clamouring for tribute under the threats of 'trick or treat', Seana couldn't help but wonder if all her scheming hadn't been in vain.

Both she and Mrs Jorgensen were busy from suppertime on, dishing out what seemed to be tons of assorted goodies to tiny witches and demons and cowboys and Indians and a host of other costumed children. Most popular of all costumes seemed to be that of a ghost, and Mrs Jorgensen claimed it was easily explained.

'It's because they can be dressed in all their warm clothing underneath the bedsheets,' she laughed, pointing to a tiny ghostie whose whiter-than-white costume was adorned with delicate pink flowers at the edges. The older woman was taking an almost childish delight in the preparations for both the children and the party to come. She, too, had been invited, and by Frank Hutton, of all people. The invitation had resulted in considerable teasing from both Seana and Ralph, but unlike Seana, Mrs Jorgensen was able to shrug off the teasing without getting one whit upset.

The invitation had forced the older woman into a massive improvisation programme that had resulted in a costume ideally suited to her matronly figure and colouring, and once the first rush of hand-outs was over, she left Seana to mind the door while she went off to change, re-emerging not long afterwards as a traditional Viking queen.

It was a handsome effort, and both Seana and her hostess were pleased by it, but it was Seana's own costume which had created the most discussion in the house. She had been forced to enlist Mrs Jorgensen's aid, but only after swearing her to absolute secrecy.

The gown was, without question, a masterpiece. Patterned after the violet one she had bought, it was in a shimmering black jersey that clung to her figure like a second skin—in those few places it got anywhere near her figure. Seana had pushed the concept to its maximum, and the result was backless, sleeveless, slit almost to the waist in front and with both sides also split to a point almost indecently high on her shapely thighs.

'It's shocking ... too shocking, if you ask me,' had been Mrs Jorgenson's first reaction.

And now, with Ralph due within minutes, Seana, too, began having second thoughts. The dress revealed far more than it could hope to conceal, and was far, far too bold for her normal taste. In fact, she suddenly realised, it was far too bold for anyone's taste.

She walked into the hallway and stared at herself in the full-length mirror, happy with every part of her costume except the dress itself. Her long hair was brushed to a gleaming lustre, almost more so than the velvet choker at her slender throat. A tiny beauty spot on one cheek completed the outward appearance of the outfit, except for a pointed witch's cap. But Seana had added a personal touch that was all her own.

It showed only when she smiled, revealing teeth blacked out to appear as pointed and fierce-looking as those of any fictional cannibal. They were, she decided, the only saving grace, the only thing that would detract from the boldness of the dress.

She heard Ralph's truck rumble to a halt outside, and suddenly turned to Mrs Jorgensen in a blind panic. 'My God!' she cried. 'I can't go through with this. I wouldn't have the nerve to carry it off, I'm sure. Oh, what am I going to do?'

'Listen to me, which is what you should have done in the first place,' was the reply as Mrs Jorgensen reached into a drawer and came up with a long, woven black shawl. 'One for every occasion,' she laughed, pinning the shawl across Seana's shoulders so that it diminished the exotic cleavage and turned the dress from over-sexed provocative to merely sexy in the time it took Ralph to ring the doorbell.

'You're a lifesaver,' Seana shouted as she flung on her coat and raced out. 'See you at the ball; and don't you dare forget your crown!'

They were halfway to the place where the ball was being held when Seana realised just how conveniently handy that shawl had been; obviously just waiting for the right moment to be added to the costume.

'You dear, sweet thing,' she murmured to herself. 'You knew all along.' And Ralph, feeling more than just a bit silly in his Roman centurion's rig, heard only the first bit and felt slightly less uncomfortable about it all.

When they arrived at the hotel where the ball was being held, Seana felt much less conspicuous about her costume. There were several young women—and a few old enough to know better—in costumes at least as revealing as hers, at least in its altered version.

On the dance floor, Seana felt almost tiny against

Ralph's comforting bulk, and she peered excitedly around the hall as they danced. Mrs Jorgensen and Frank Hutton arrived about half an hour later, and there were a few other people Seana knew. But nowhere in the growing crowd was there the slightest hint of carrot-red beard or eyes like green glass. It appeared her preparations were in vain after all.

By eleven o'clock Seana was exhausted from dancing so much, and was glad of the respite when the band took a break.

She joined Mrs Jorgensen and some of the other ladies, many of whom were lightly teasing her friend about the obvious change in temperament revealed by her date.

'Do I detect a romance in the offing?' Seana laughed, joining in the friendly teasing. 'I'm absolutely certain I saw Frank smile at least once tonight.'

'Don't start leaping before you look,' Mrs Jorgensen retorted. 'You know what jumping to conclusions can lead to. And I see your own bit of scheming has gone awry, unless of course you've changed your mind and decided that Ralph's a safer bet than Ryan.'

Half an hour and several glasses of rather potent punch later, she wasn't so sure. The dancing was becoming livelier as the witching hour approached, and Ralph's appreciation of her costume was becoming uncomfortably evident. Then, during the short lull between numbers, a redheaded girl in a green harem outfit made her entrance, and Seana stopped worrying about her own costume's boldness.

The newcomer would have been six foot tall in her flat-heeled slippers, and she was proportionately large . . . everywhere. Seana felt Ralph, beside her, stiffen to attention as he noticed the redhead, and there was a tangible current of awareness that seemed to flow like magic through the masculine element of the crowd. A moment later there was another flow of emotion, this time from the females in the room, and it was pure and simple green-eyed envy.

Ralph recovered, she thought, flatteringly quickly, but she brushed aside his quiet apology. 'Don't apologise,' she replied. 'I can't say I blame you a bit. That's one of the most striking women I've ever seen.'

And truly the junoesque redhead seemed the answer to the masculine dream; she was beautiful, poised, classically lovely. But there was so much of her it was almost overwhelming.

Ralph whispered into Seana's ear as he summed up the male viewpoint, and she almost laughed out loud at the correctness of his analogy. 'She's like a prize-winning piece of livestock,' Ralph whispered. 'The kind of thing you trot out to exhibit to visitors. I can just imagine sitting in front of a great stone fireplace in my dream mansion. I'd whistle and my dog would come and sit by my side, then I'd whistle again and *she* would come out and sit at the other side. Pure status symbol.'

'That's ridiculous,' Seana snorted, but she knew as she protested that he had pinpointed the situation exactly.

Ralph turned her away on to the dance floor again as the musicians got their breath and once again began to play, and when they had circled back to where the redhead was, Seana missed a step and had to clutch at Ralph's shoulder to keep from falling.

The magnificent exhibit, the status symbol, was no longer alone. And the man with her, unmistakable despite his costume, was Ryan Stranger!

But this Ryan Stranger was no one Seana knew. Piece by piece, his costume was merely that, but altogether it somehow seemed real, terrifyingly real. He was transformed, and the new Ryan was the com-

plete pirate, even to the patch which covered one eye.
The remaining eye glared hotly around the room with
a haughty, arrogant, almost belligerent assurance.

One hand rested on the sword at his belt; the other
clutched a length of gold chain that linked him to the
neck of the junoesque harem girl, claiming her, announcing to the entire crowd that she was his captive.
His!

Seana felt sick inside. All her scheming now seemed
only a childish dream, as futile as the dream she had
been consciously cherishing that Ryan might actually
care for her. His commanding presence now denied
the assurances Mrs Jorgensen had given her, and Seana
felt cheap at having gone to such extremes to attract
Ryan's attention.

How could I compete with that? she wondered. It's
like comparing a pick-up truck to a limousine, and I'd
be an even worse fool to try.

Then she realised that the pirate chieftain's single
eye had become fixed on *her*. And worse, he was forg-
ing a path through the dancers, the harem girl captive
trailing behind him on her golden chain.

Seana shuddered, every instinct warning her to flee.
But it was too late already. And Ryan knew it, too.
Knew it, and was pleased.

Seana could only nod as Ryan introduced the tall
redhead, wishing she could smile but suddenly not
daring to because of her blacked-out teeth. Veronica
Landsdowne, suffering no such difficulty, revealed
glistening, even teeth. Close up, she was even more
beautiful than at a distance, with rich brown eyes and
a complexion like cream. The skimpiness of her costume revealed a truly superb figure, and she carried
herself like a born courtesan despite the chain of
ownership around her neck.

'Well, I see you did turn into a witch,' Ryan

observed, his bold eye raking Seana from her pointed shoes to the little pointed cap on her head. She felt about ten years old beneath his gaze, so insecure did his companion make her feel, and all her defensiveness roused at his words.

'Would you have preferred a pumpkin?' she asked, knowing she sounded ridiculous talking with her mouth shut. But she was damned if she'd open it now, not with all that goop on her teeth.

He laughed, and the mockery was there, as usual, ringing its jeering assault upon her ears. 'A pumpkin would be just a little too much out of character, lady-bug,' he chuckled, then handed the golden chain to Ralph in an invitation the wildlife officer was quick to accept. And before Seana could think to object, Ryan's arm was fast about her own waist, pulling her against him as he sifted them into the madly whirling dancers.

His lips were butterflies against her ear as he held her closely and spun smoothly into the throng, and Seana didn't even have to think to follow his skilled steps. She had enough trouble just catching her breath, especially after he began to whisper to her.

'I should have known you wouldn't wait for me tonight,' his voice rasped. 'You're a woman of little faith, ladybug.'

'And you're a conceited, arrogant so-and-so if you expected me to wait on the basis of a three-week-old maybe,' she gasped in reply. 'Not that you really expected me to, seeing you obviously made sure you were well taken care of.'

His laugh was hollow, mocking. 'Jealous? I'll have to be careful or you'll turn me into a frog or something.'

'A skunk would be more appropriate,' Seana retorted. 'And you're holding me much too tightly. Your slave girl might appreciate such treatment, but I don't, thank you.'

'Ahah! You *are* jealous,' he replied, making absolutely no concession to her demand to be held less tightly.

'I am not!' she lied.

'Don't be ashamed of it; I might be too, if I was you,' he chuckled. 'Who knows? Maybe *I'm* jealous of Ralph—you never stopped to think of that, did you?'

'Certainly not. I've never heard anything so ridiculous,' she whispered. 'And *stop* that!' as his lips nuzzled her ear in what could only be a form of caress.

'Stop . . . what?' he murmured. And his lips shifted down to trace feathers of delight along the length of her neck. His left hand held firmly as she tried to pull her hand free, and his right was a living flame along the smoothness of her back as it crept beneath the shawl.

Seana felt as if she would melt, held upright only by her growing anger. How dared he so deliberately set out to arouse her, caress her so . . . so intimately? Intimately . . . and worse, she realised; the intimacy was nothing when compared to the success he was enjoying. Her entire body seemed to throb at his touch, to become totally sensitive to his chest against her heaving breasts, his thigh as he pressed against her in the turns.

The music stopped not a moment too soon, and with her last vestige of willpower she thrust herself away from him. She didn't trust herself any more to speak, or even to look at him.

The sound was barely audible, but the feeling at her midriff halted her in mid-step, and she looked down to see the strands of her shawl intricately enmeshed in the design of Ryan's sword-belt. She looked up then to find him grinning down at her, aware of her predicament and enjoying it immensely.

'You'd better hope the next dance is a slow one,' he said. 'Otherwise you're going to have problems.'

'I already have problems,' she hissed. 'Will you please do something?'

'Of course,' he replied, and pulled her into his arms again as the music began once more. This time he left her enough room so that she could try and untangle herself, but his very nearness seemed to make her fingers like lumps of lead, totally incapable of unsnarling the threads. There were tears of sheer frustration in her eyes when he finally moved her fingers away and shifted his own hands in between their slowly moving bodies.

Seana was forced to dance then with both arms upheld around his neck, her eyes level with his brow as he moved with head bent, his fingers at work unravelling the shawl.

'Wouldn't it be easier to do this standing still?' she hissed, feeling that everyone was staring at them. Certainly *she* was aware of his fingers as they touched her bare skin at the bottom of the gown's deep neckline, and it seemed to her as though everyone else should notice as well.

'Easier,' he agreed, 'but not nearly so much fun.' And his fingers slid inside the neckline, running like flames across her lower ribs, then up to tease the nipple of one breast.

Seana gasped, first with shock at his boldness, then with a moan of desire as her body responded. His caress couldn't have lasted two seconds, but it established beyond question his control both of her and of the situation.

'You're not the only one who can play bewitching games tonight, ladybug,' he hissed, then lifted his head to rivet her with that single blazing eye as he moved his lips down to cover her mouth in a kiss both brief and arousing. His lips seemed to reach for her very soul, branding her, making her every bit as much his captive as the slave girl in the harem costume.

'You're free, by the way,' he whispered as

he teasingly released her mouth.

Seana pulled abruptly away, but her gasp of relief became one of shock as he lifted his hands so that she slipped straight out from beneath the shawl. Then his arm was round her again, pulling her close as he did a quick shift in step that brought them next to Mrs Jorgensen and her partner.

'Yours, I believe,' he grinned, and draped the shawl across its rightful owner's shoulder before spinning Seana away even as her fingers reached for it.

She could feel the cool air on the deep cleavage he had exposed, but only for an instant. Then there was only the burning warmth of his chest against hers, the fusing of their bodies, the touch of his hands at her waist, his fingers softly stroking desire up and down her spine.

It was a slow, deliberate arousal of her entire body, and although her mind recognised that, her body paid no heed to it . . . only to Ryan and his touch. But Seana could move her lips, and when she'd pleaded with him long enough, he released her.

She spun out of his arms and fled like a startled doe, weaving through the crowd of dancers in a panicky dash for the powder room, where she halted just inside the door and stood panting, afraid she would be ill.

'You'd better let me help you,' said a voice from behind her as the door swung open to admit Ryan's harem girl, a worried look on her face. She led Seana to where she could sit down, then dabbled a paper towel in some water and bent down to sponge Seana's brow.

'I'll . . . I'll be all right,' Seana gasped, her breast still heaving as if she had run a mile.

'You won't be if you don't learn to handle Ryan Stranger better than that,' was the unexpected reply. 'Does he always affect you like this, or is tonight something special?'

'I . . . usually he just makes me angry,' Seana confessed, then wondered what in the world she was doing confiding in this woman, of all people.

The redhead raised an eyebrow and shook her head sadly. 'I'd say you're lucky he didn't take you over his knee, but then he's probably still in a state of shock. It's probably the first time in his life that a woman has ever stood *him* up.'

Seana gaped at her, unable to comprehend, much less believe what she had just heard.

'I don't understand,' she said. '*Who* stood him up?'

'Well, I presume it was you,' came the astonishing reply. 'Unless he's got some other girl-friend named Seana. You're a braver girl than I am, let me tell you. When we stopped to collect you and he found you'd gone . . . well, I wouldn't have wanted to be in your shoes at that moment, and that's a fact.'

'But . . . but I didn't stand him up,' Seana protested, still not quite understanding what had been told to her. 'Unless . . .' and her anger flared like a torch at the thought '. . . unless he expected me to be waiting at the door on the basis of his suggestion that he'd see me tonight . . . *maybe*! And if that's what he thought, then it's just too damned bad!'

She was on her feet, all ready to rush back out and have it out with Ryan then and there, but the redhead's hand on her arm restrained her.

'Look, I don't know about his suggestions,' Veronica cautioned, 'but before you go off half-cocked you'd better know that I *do* know he sent you a message last week to make the date for tonight. I know he did, because my husband and I were both standing right there when he did it.'

Husband! It was a toss-up which was the greater surprise, the fact that Veronica was not, as Seana had reckoned, Ryan's date for the evening, or the proof that he had sent her a message—one she'd never received.

'True,' said Veronica. 'He was afraid we wouldn't get out until the last minute, so he asked a trucker he knew to phone you and let you know.'

Seana sank back into the seat, her knees suddenly unable to support her. 'But . . . but I never got any phone call,' she said. 'I wouldn't have . . . oh, what difference does it make now? He wouldn't believe me anyway.'

'Well, he sure won't if you don't even tell him,' said Veronica. 'And what's it going to hurt? He's cooled down a lot or he wouldn't even have danced with you, I'd imagine, much less send me in here to make sure you were okay.'

'Ryan sent you?' Seana was surprised and it must have showed on her face.

'That's right. I think he was going to send your friend Mrs . . . oh, the lady with the white hair. But she was being wooed rather vigorously, to use Ryan's words, so he sent me instead. And now that I've done my good deed for the day, I think I'll go see if I can find my husband. You're sure you can cope?'

'Oh . . . yes, I'm fine . . . now,' Seana smiled, then laughed as Veronica shrank back at the sight of her blackened teeth. 'Awful, aren't they?' she giggled. 'They were supposed to be a surprise for Ryan, but I think I'll clean them before I go out in case he's not in the mood for any more surprises.'

She did so quickly, then almost pranced back into the ballroom, she felt so much better. Ralph was seated with Mrs Jorgensen and Frank Hutton, but there wasn't a sign of Ryan, and Ralph's reply to Seana's query was like a slap in the face.

'He's gone. And I don't blame him a bit. That was a dirty trick and I'm not pleased at being involved in it,' he said.

CHAPTER NINE

'GONE? But he can't be! I have to explain,' Seana said blankly, her soul going cold at the very thought of Ryan leaving without her even having a chance to tell him what had happened.

She started towards the door, only to be halted by Ralph's hand at her elbow. 'You won't catch him now,' he said. 'The way he went out of here, he'll be halfway back to the Kakwa by now. Why don't you try explaining to me instead? I think I deserve it almost as much.'

Seana, for the first time, looked at Ralph, seeing the anger hidden beneath the surface as he struggled to hang on to his temper. A glance at Mrs Jorgensen brought the surprising revelation that she, too, thought that Seana had deliberately used Ralph in an attempt to get at Ryan.

'I . . . I know what you must be thinking,' she said numbly, allowing Ralph to lead her into a chair. 'But I didn't get any message from Ryan. I didn't know a thing about it until Veronica mentioned it to me just a few minutes ago. And that's the truth!' she added, her heart stricken by the looks of censure she had been getting. 'Veronica said he sent a message with a trucker, but I never got it. I *didn't*!'

'It's true, unless she's a better actress than I think she is,' said a voice from behind them, and Veronica slid into a vacant chair before introducing her husband, an American businessman who had hunted with Ryan for several seasons and was a close friend.

'But he did send the message,' said the man. 'Both

of us were right there when he did it.' He went on to describe the trucker to whom Ryan had entrusted the suddenly-significant message, whereupon Ralph burst out with an oath that fairly shook the room.

'Hell!' he cried. 'I know now why you didn't get it. I arrested that joker halfway to town after I caught him poaching. He was in court that same afternoon and after the fine he had thrown at him, I'm not surprised he didn't remember anything about Ryan's message.'

Vindicated, but no happier because of it, Seana could only sit in numbed sorrow as everyone commiserated. It was all very nice, but it accomplished nothing to solve the problem. Ryan was gone, probably for the remainder of the hunting season, since Veronica's husband said he was fully booked out.

'Maybe if I drove down there . . .' she suggested hopefully as they were driving home, the party having lost most of its gaiety because of the mix-up.

'Not a chance,' said Ralph. 'His base camp is so far back in the bush you couldn't get within fifty miles. I'm not even sure *I'll* be seeing him.'

He offered to try and send a radio message to Ryan, who would have a radio link in case of emergencies, but Seana vetoed that possibility. 'No, there've been enough mix-ups already,' she insisted. 'If you can't see him personally, I'll . . . I'll just have to wait until he returns and explain it myself. In·fact that might be the best thing anyway.'

'All right, whatever you say,' Ralph agreed. 'But I want your promise that you *will* explain it—first thing, before you two get involved in one of your never-ending feuds.' And he snorted disgustedly. 'Frankly, I think you're both a couple of dopes. Everybody can see you're in love with each other, but Ryan's too stubborn to admit it and you're too stupid to shut up and give him a chance.'

'I just wish I could believe it was that simple,' Seana replied, hoping her voice didn't betray the singing in her heart. Could it really be possible? Or was Ralph just reading something into his friend's behaviour and making his own interpretations?

The thought of trying to explain to Ryan about his message—more than a month after the fact—was something she tried hard to avoid during the following weeks. Instead, she accepted that it would have to be done, prayed almost every night that Ralph would find an opportunity to do the worst part of it for her, and concentrated on having Ryan's manuscript completed by the time the guiding season ended.

But with less than a week to go, she finally had to admit defeat on the manuscript. There were just too many things that couldn't progress without Ryan's personal attention. She was also finding concentration difficult as her day of reckoning drew closer, and she was missing Mrs Jorgensen and the older woman's advice and support.

Even the regular flow of postcards couldn't make up for that lack, although from the anecdotes on them, Mrs Jorgensen was having a wonderful time in Europe.

It wasn't that Seana was particularly lonely; her job and Ryan's manuscript kept her busy and she saw Ralph on the few occasions he wasn't busy working. But the coming confrontation with Ryan preyed on her mind, so much so that even Frank Hutton commented on her moodiness.

Her delight was overwhelming, then, when Ralph came in to announce that he had finally got in to Ryan's main camp, and that the issue of the missing message was now resolved. 'And I'm damned glad of it, too,' he said. 'I can make enough enemies without having

Ryan turn into one just because of something like that.'

'But what did he say?' Seana kept asking. 'When is he finishing up? When will he be back? Is he still angry with me?'

'That, my dear, is something you'll have to sort out for yourself,' Ralph replied. 'Obviously he'll be back after the last day of the season, but he didn't send any specific message, probably for fear I'd lose it.'

'He didn't send any message at all?' Seana's heart was flashing danger signals and she felt strangely lightheaded. It wasn't all resolved then, despite what Ralph had said. Or, she wondered, was it indeed resolved, with her completely out of the picture?

'Only that we'll all have to have dinner together before I leave. I've been transferred, finally, and I'll be going in as number one man at Red Deer right after Christmas.'

He made the comment lightly, but Seana knew how much he had been angling for that particular transfer, which meant a substantial promotion. 'Oh, how wonderful for you!' she smiled, and meant it, despite the immediate sadness at losing such a good friend.

Her own problems were shoved to the background as they discussed Ralph's transfer and his plans involving it, and it wasn't until he had left that Seana began to wonder once more about the lack of a personal message from Ryan.

The final day of hunting season was only a week away, however, and she felt certain she could hold out that long. And she did, but at the expense of jangled nerves and a constant, growing tension that threw an ache into her back and had her so jumpy by the final day of the season that Frank Hutton sent her home early and with a fierce demonstration of his own temper.

'Take a hot shower and three aspirins. Take a cold

shower. Shoot yourself, for all I care,' he said. 'But don't come back into my office until you've straightened out.'

He brushed aside her attempts at apology, and once she was home, guilt quickly gave way to anticipation. At least she would have time to properly prepare for Ryan's return.

She spent the rest of the afternoon baking and laying the groundwork for a gourmet dinner, then did her fingernails, had a shower and washed her hair, dithered for nearly an hour over what to wear, did her nails again. And still she was ready far too early. It was barely dark, which meant Ryan couldn't be there for a couple of hours at least.

Seana spent that time pondering over what she would say to him, inventing complicated scenarios and then rejecting her own lines as either juvenile, soppy, or just plain ridiculous. But by ten o'clock even that was wearing thin, and at eleven she ate half of her gourmet dinner and flung the rest in the garbage in a fit of pique. She was in bed at midnight, but didn't get to sleep until nearly three in the morning, her ears so finely tuned to the noise of each passing vehicle that she came bolt upright in the bed if any so much as seemed to slow down.

Work the next morning was a torment, and it got worse when she overheard some forestry people talking during coffee break. It was impossible to catch every word, but the ones she did hear were enough to make her bad temper of the day before seem mild indeed by comparison to the way she felt at the moment.

Her first words when Ryan stepped into the Forestry office emerged without thought or planning; they were a simply emotional example of exactly how she felt. And they fairly dripped with venom distilled by hurt and anger.

'So they finally let you out of jail, did they?'

Ryan sauntered forward far enough to lean with one hand on the corner of her desk before answering, and then he didn't really answer at all.

'You're sure cheerful this morning. Which side of the bed did you get out of?'

'That, Mr Stranger, is none of your business,' she snapped. 'None at all.'

'It sure as hell *is* my business, if you're going to take all your frustrations out on me,' he retorted, and his eyes gleamed with the first fierce light of the battle to come.

'You're actually proud of yourself, aren't you?' she countered. 'Arrested for common, drunken brawling—and you're proud of it . . . just about what I'd expect from you!'

Ryan flinched, obviously a flinch of guilt, Seana saw, but there was no guilt in his words when he snapped back at her, his voice raised to match the timbre of her own.

'I certainly don't *think* I'm proud of it,' he said coldly, 'but I don't see that it's any business of yours if I am. Who do you think you are . . . my mother?'

'Not . . . at . . . any . . . price,' she replied, the words slowly and deliberately spaced for maximum chill.

'Well, we've got that much settled, anyway,' he sneered. His eyes had turned a darker-than-usual green and his lips had a taut, angry thinness. 'So unless you've married me when I wasn't looking, you've got no damned business questioning my actions at all, have you?'

Seana didn't . . . couldn't reply. The truth was self-evident and unarguable. Ryan didn't take her silence for acceptance, however, but cocked his head in thought as he stared at her through icy eyes.

'Ah, now I understand,' he said mockingly. 'You're

all snarly because I didn't come calling last night. And you heard on the radio this morning about half a dozen guides getting busted for drinking, and as usual you jumped to conclusions. Well, let me tell you something, *Miss* Muldoon. I don't know what the hell you're talking about.'

He paused, giving her every chance to apologise, to say anything, but Seana's stunned mind refused to function.

'As a matter of fact, I *was* going to call on you last night, but I couldn't make it back in time. And judging from this performance, Miss Muldoon, I'm just as glad I didn't. Hell, if a little bit of typing and kiss or two makes you this possessive, what in hell would marriage do? You'd be wanting to hold my hand when I went to the bathroom!'

That was too much. The apology that had been on Seana's lips was lost in the flash of her own temper. 'I wouldn't marry you if they were giving you away in pairs,' she snapped.

'Wait until you're asked,' he replied, his own temper as hot as hers.

'Don't bother,' she sneered. 'And as for your precious typing, you know what you can do with that . . .'

'Oh . . . no!' The anger in his face was altered by a stern, stubborn determination. 'We've got an agreement about that and I'm holding you to it. And now, if you don't mind, dear Miss Muldoon, I'm going off to find my friend Ralph, who at the very least won't scream at me like a fishwife as soon as I walk in the door.'

And Seana was left, half standing and half sitting, her mouth goldfishing in mute rage as he strode through the door and slammed it so hard the glass trembled. Then she, too, was trembling, mostly with anger at herself.

How could I possibly be so stupid? she wondered. It was all ruined now, and beyond doubt it was her own fault. She owed Ryan not one simple apology, but two, and the second was far from simple.

One thing was certain, she had never seen Ryan so angry. If his mood continued until he found Ralph, she was sure to hear more about it that evening, when she and Ralph were going out for dinner to celebrate his transfer.

'And *he'll* probably shout at me too,' she thought ruefully as she stepped out of the shower and started getting ready. She was ready, as usual, on time, wearing a soft gold blouse and a skirt of black silk with a fine gold thread woven through it.

But he didn't arrive at eight o'clock, which rather surprised her, because Ralph, unlike Ryan, was usually very punctual. And when he hadn't arrived by eight-thirty, she began to wonder if the two men hadn't decided on some unique form of revenge, but a knock at the door a moment later made her thrust away such unkind thoughts. Carefully wiping the scowl from her face, she ran to open the door, and the first thing she saw was a huge bouquet of flowers.

'Oh!' she cried delightedly, then raised her eyes to meet the mocking appraisal of Ryan Stranger.

'Very lovely,' he said, making no attempt to disguise the admiration in his voice.

'Oh,' Seana said again, then stammered in her confusion, 'Er . . . come in, please. Ralph will be here in a moment, I should imagine. Would you . . . er . . . like a drink or something?'

'No, thanks; we're already late,' he said. 'My fault, which probably shows I shouldn't try to stand in for somebody as punctual as Ralph. He was . . . called away on a final anti-poaching mission, so I came instead.'

Seana stood there, silent, and before she realised what was happening, Ryan had lifted her coat from the closet and was placing it around her shoulders. He took the flowers out of her nerveless fingers and laid them down on the sideboard. 'They'll keep,' he said. 'Shall we go?'

And suddenly she was sitting in his truck, aware somehow that it was washed and polished and clean inside, but less certain of how she'd got there.

Neither of them spoke for the first few moments, but it was Ryan who broke the silence, in a voice so soft Seana barely heard him.

'What did you say?' she asked, unsure she had heard it correctly.

'I said I was sorry about this morning.'

'Oh.' Unaccountably, his apology served only to bring back hostile memories, and she had to bite her tongue to keep her temper in. She counted to ten, slowly, before continuing.

'I'm sorry too. And really, it was my fault.' She thought the admission would choke her, but amazingly, once it was out, she felt several pounds lighter and not choked up at all.

'Umm-hmm.' That took a moment to soak in, and then she had to bite her tongue again, but still the start of her retort slipped past.

'What? You . . . you . . .' She began to splutter before it got worse, but Ryan was already interrupting.

'. . . nice fellow. Splendid fellow, even. After all, I did apologise, even if it wasn't my fault, which you've admitted. Besides, I brought you flowers, didn't I?'

She turned to find his eyes laughing at her, and though she knew it was the cue for her to laugh too, his mockery only made her more angry.

'Take me home, please,' she demanded.

'Why?' His voice was innocuously bland. Suspiciously so.

'Because it's obvious if you and I stay together we're going to end up fighting,' she said acidly, 'and I'd rather it wasn't in public.'

'Okay.' His reply was curiously soft, but he turned the truck right at the next corner, away from downtown, and Seana closed her eyes and relaxed in what she saw as a major victory. Then she opened them again and realised that while they were no longer headed downtown, they weren't going to Mrs Jorgensen's, either.

'Where are you going?' she asked in sudden, suspicious confusion.

'Where we can have dinner—and fight—without making a public spectacle of it,' he replied, still softly.

'What? Just a minute . . . you can't . . . I won't . . .' Seana was stammering and knew it.

'Seana . . . please just *shut up!*' And there was a deadly calm about the way he said it. She sat. What else could she do . . . they had passed the city limits and she wasn't about to jump from a truck going sixty miles an hour down a highway in the darkness.

They passed Clairmont, and a few minutes later passed the highway fringe of Sexsmith, whereupon Ryan ignored the next curve in the highway and sent the truck straight ahead along a narrow gravel road, the old, original highway into the Saddle Hills, Seana realised, and wondered if he could be heading for White Mountain Tower by some unknown route.

But a few miles farther, he swung on to an even narrower, snow-choked track leading into the edge of the hills, a track so deeply rutted he had to force the truck on in its lowest gears to manoeuvre the steep inclines.

The road finally ended in the yard of a small farm, but Ryan switched off the headlights before Seana caught more than a glimpse of a large, rambling log cabin and outbuildings of the same material. Leaving the truck running, he flung open his door and stepped down into the snow.

'Stay here; I'll be back in a minute.' It was a command she couldn't disobey. She had no confidence in her ability to handle the heavy truck, even presuming she could have got it turned around in the first place. She sat, silent and wondering, as she saw a glimmer of lamplight spark within the house. The doorway became a small, lighted rectangle through which Ryan's shadow drifted as he crossed the yard and returned to the vehicle. Seconds later he was opening the passenger door and lifting her into his arms.

'What? You . . . you put me down!' she cried, wriggling to get free. He merely ignored her, stomping carefully through the deep snow and kicking open the door. Once inside, he set her gently down on the dry floor. Then he shrugged off his heavy coat and led her over to where a fire, newly born, was clawing its way through the kindling in a huge stone fireplace.

'You'd better leave your coat on for a few minutes, although it won't take long to warm up,' he said. 'Would you like a drink?'

Seana stood, staring into the flames as she tried to interpret the curious tone in his voice. 'Yes, I think I would, actually,' she said at last. 'Brandy, please. But where are we?' The words all seemed to run together.

'Home.' Ryan threw the word over his shoulder as he busied himself mixing drinks. Seana, chilly despite her coat, moved closer to the fire and perched on the edge of a large, old-fashioned chair near the edge of the hearth. She looked up as he crossed the room with the drinks on a small tray, and suddenly realised that this was a Ryan Stranger she had never seen before. There was none of his usual rough-hewn casualness;

his hair was neatly combed, his moustache and beard trimmed close, if still curly. His shirt was of a soft, pale green that picked out the highlights in the perfectly-knotted tie. And his suit, she realised with a start, was perfectly cut and exceptionally expensive.

Suddenly as warm as she had been cool only seconds before, she rose to throw off her coat, but halted at his commanding look.

Wordlessly, he set the tray on a coffee table, took her coat politely and left the room with it. Seana picked up her drink and was seated again when he returned.

Ryan lifted his own glass in a silent toast, smiling brightly at her, then turned his attention to the flickering fire, which cast more light into the room than came from the single coal-oil lantern on another table in the corner.

They sat, each staring into the flames, until the drinks were finished. Then Ryan silently refilled the glasses, and when he brought Seana's to her, said quietly, 'It'll be a few minutes before dinner. You don't mind if I leave you here?'

She nodded silently and turned to stare into the flames again as he left, quietly closing the door behind him. Then, curious, she left the drink and wandered slowly through the huge room. The walls, contrary to her first impressions, were not log, but softly polished planks of what appeared to be maple. An ancient rifle hung above the mantel, along with a pistol of equal vintage and a weird, unusually attractive painting that looked like a section of cave wall with a crude, primitive, wolf-like figure dominating it. As she moved through the room, her eyes kept returning to the painting, though she was unsure why it so attracted her.

The furniture was a blend of heavy, solid old pieces and newer, apparently hand-made fixtures that also radiated solidarity. The floor was covered in various skins, including one of a huge grizzly bear, and there were the massive antlers of deer, moose and elk on the walls.

The bar where Ryan had mixed the drinks also appeared to be hand-crafted, matching some of the other newer furniture.

Returning to the fire, she picked up her drink again and stood silently staring at the wolf painting, drawn to it, absorbed by the primitive subtlety. She didn't hear the door open behind her.

'Do you like it?'

Seana turned, startled for an instant; then she calmed. 'Yes, I rather think I do. It's certainly unusual . . . rather compelling, in a way.'

'It was done by a guy who used to be a towerman, down on Copton Tower. He's an art instructor at the college now, I think. That painting is the only thing of its type he ever did, to my knowledge, and I bought it before the paint was hardly dry. Now I think he specialises in pen sketches that are very popular and very expensive, but nothing like this.'

They both stood admiring the painting for a moment, then Ryan said, 'We'd best go in to dinner now, or your soup will get cold.'

They moved into a dining room that was nearly as large as the room they had just left, but lit only by a trio of candlesticks on the enormous maple table. A set of café doors, Seana noticed, led to a kitchen where, rather to her surprise, normal electric lights were obviously in use.

'Generally I prefer the light from the lamps and the fire,' Ryan told her as he seated her.

'What are you doing, reading my mind?' she asked, startled by the accuracy of his remark.

'It's not hard, usually,' he replied with a slow grin,

picking up his soup spoon and dipping it into the bowl in front of him. The soup was a clear, subtly-spiced consommé with tiny croutons floating in it. They both ate slowly, still not saying anything, and when the soup was done Ryan took her plate and shouldered his way through to the kitchen.

There's no way *that* came out of a can, Seana thought to herself. You're just full of surprises tonight, aren't you?

The main course was even more astounding, and she felt twinges of jealousy when it was placed before her—succulent chunks of pork tenderloin, broiled on a skewer and then smothered on a bed of rice by a tangy peanut sauce. She closed her eyes and inhaled the delicate aroma as it tantalised her taste-buds.

Ryan opened some excellent wine to accompany the satay, but still kept silent as he watched Seana tuck into the meal with undeniable enthusiasm.

'That was delicious,' she said when only a denuded plate was left in front of her. 'What did you just *whip up* for dessert, crêpes suzettes?'

Ryan raised one eyebrow sceptically at her sarcasm, but said only, 'Not quite. I haven't got to that part of the book yet.'

She shrank back inside herself, cursing her viperish tongue as he asked, 'Would you settle for mince pie and ice cream?'

'No ice cream, thanks, but if the pie is half as good as what I've eaten so far, I'll have an extra-large helping.' Redemption? Impossible to tell anything from those fathomless green eyes. He was silent as he picked up the dishes and moved silently through to the kitchen, emerging a minute later with the pie. It was, she decided after the first bite, quite definitely up to his established standard.

They returned to the living room for coffee and

liqueurs, and Seana sat pensively while Ryan stirred
up the fire and placed a few fresh logs on it. He offered
her a cigarette, only smiled at her refusal, then spent
what seemed like forever in filling, tamping and finally
lighting a pipe from the rack beside his own chair. And
even after that he didn't say anything, and the silence
was wearing on Seana's nerves.

She began to fidget, shifting in her chair, crossing
and uncrossing her ankles and peering idly about the
dim room.

He certainly wasn't going to make it easy for her,
she decided. He just sat, appraising her through
hooded, speculative eyes. And after a few minutes it
was no longer really an appraisal, but something of a
caress, bold and yet gentle, obvious and yet so subtle.

'Say something, damn it!' she finally exploded.
'Don't just sit there undressing me with those insolent
eyes. Say something! Tell me why I'm here. Tell me
what you *want*!'

Ryan merely raised one eyebrow, watching her until
she ran down, until the words ran out.

'How many children would you like?'

'What . . . what kind of a question is that?' she
demanded after the moment it took for his words to
sink in.

'A fairly simple one, I would have thought,' he
replied gently. 'And one I very much expect an answer
to, unless of course you're planning on moving to Red
Deer with Ralph.'

Seana cocked her head, then turned away from his
eyes, staring into the kaleidoscope of the fire. She
wanted to answer, but dared not; she couldn't trust
her mouth. Yet she must say something, and what
finally came out was, 'Why do you want to know?'

'I thought *I* was asking the questions,' he replied
calmly, still in that soft, deceptively gentle fashion. But

he had raised that eyebrow again, rousing the suspicion inside her. He was playing with her, and she was afraid.

'I'm not sure it's any of your business,' she said, then continued before he could say anything, 'but no, of course I'm not going with Ralph.'

There, it was said, but had she also revealed the depth of her feelings for Ryan himself? Dared she? Her only guide was that hateful lifted eyebrow and a smug curling of his lip.

'Just as well,' he said finally. 'He's too nice a guy; I don't think I'd wish *you* on him.' Mocking laughter in the eyes now, and Seana felt her temper rising to meet the mockery. She bit her tongue.

'Well, thank you very much! And if that's all you have to say, I think perhaps I'd like to go home now.'

'What? Without doing the dishes?' He laughed openly at her, rising lithely to his feet to stand before her, his stature that of a predatory cat. 'Surely Mother Jorgensen taught you better manners than that. And if she didn't—I will!'

He was already reaching for her when she snarled, 'You just be careful . . . I bite!' Strong words from a girl who was cowering in her seat as if confronted by the devil.

'Sure you do,' he grinned, and then his hands were on her shoulders, lifting her from the chair like a broken doll as he bent to capture her mouth with his own, kissing her with a fierceness that first frightened her, then began to play on her passion, rousing her despite her objections.

His lips were like searing irons as they scorched across her mouth, her cheeks, then down into the neckline of her blouse, burning across the tops of her breasts. Seana wanted to fight him, but her body was already in surrender, her arms flung around his neck and every fibre of her straining against him, savouring the hardness of him against her.

Then, as suddenly as it had begun, it was over, and she opened her eyes to find herself snuggled tightly in against his muscular neck. 'You still haven't answered my question,' he grated, 'and you will, you know, so why not get it over with?'

The lobe of his ear was only inches from her swollen lips, and she didn't even stop to think before her teeth nipped at it, not viciously, but enough to sting.

Ryan grunted at the sudden pain, then thrust her away from him, his fingers like steel claws around her upper arms. His eyes glowed like the coals in the fire, and when he released one of her arms from one white-knuckled hand, she thought for a second he was going to strike her.

Then the harsh lights faded from his eyes and he let go her other arm, stepping away from her with exaggerated caution. 'All right,' he said. 'You can do the dishes first.'

He led the way into the enormous and perfectly-planned kitchen, a veritable chef's paradise with every possible convenience.

'You can wash,' he said. And a moment later she was elbow-deep in dishwater, with Ryan standing beside her and drying the things as they emerged.

But when she started to scrub at the first pot, he took it from her and laughed. 'Leave that,' he said, shaking his head. 'It's no problem.'

'Don't be silly,' she replied. 'The pots and pans are always the worst, especially if you leave them overnight.'

'So throw them in the dishwasher.' The words were very soft, his voice deadpan, but the laughter was there in his eyes and in the curve of his lip. Seana turned to face him, unable to believe she had heard him right. But yes, there was a dishwasher, although how she had missed seeing it before, she couldn't imagine.

'You ... you tricked me,' she cried, 'and what's more, you did it deliberately! Just as you always do.' Lifting her soapy hands from the sink, she snatched the tea-towel from his hands and scrubbed at her fingers as if they were covered in syrup.

When he took her gently by the shoulders, she began to flail at him with her fists, but it was like striking them against solid wood.

'Only because I love you,' he said in the midst of her assault, so softly she thought she must be hearing things.

'What did you say?' she asked, stopping with both fists still raised before her.

'I said I love you, but you couldn't expect me to marry you until I've seen how you shape up in the kitchen,' he replied gravely. 'We can't spend all our time in bed, after all.'

'You ... love me?' The words came out, but she was only half aware she'd uttered them as a question. The sound of her heart rushing, laughing, alive again, overshadowed all else.

'Well, of course I love you. Surely you don't think I'd put up with you otherwise?' He bent to kiss her softly on the lips before she could reply. 'And don't get stroppy with me, ladybug. It cost me an arm and a leg to buy Ralph off so that I could organise this evening, and I have no intention of spending any more of it arguing.'

'Yes, sir,' she replied, raising her lips willingly, greedily, to meet his. There was no violence in his kisses then, only the sweetness of unity as their lips met, as her arms stole around his neck to let her fingers tangle in the dark red curls.

His arms closed around her, his hands moving over her body in a symphony of delight that roused her not to surrender, but to the edges of fulfilment. When he carried her to the bedroom, her body was light as air, her mind almost adrift with the intoxication of wanting him, needing him, and . . . finally . . . having him.

Later, her entire being awash with the afterglow of loving, she asked quietly. 'Do you still want to know how many children I want?'

'I think we'd better get the wedding organised first,' he grinned. 'Then we can just take them as they come; we've plenty of time . . . all the rest of our lives.'

Seana sighed, lying back against the curve of his arm as she let her fingers romp through the curly hair on his chest and stomach.

'There might be a slight delay about the wedding,' she said hesitantly. 'I . . . I sort of promised Mrs Jorgensen I wouldn't get married without her being there. It was only a joke, but she won't be back for another four months.'

'We'll get married at Christmas; that gives us just enough time to organise.' He was adamant, no give in his voice at all.

'But . . . but what about Mrs Jorgensen?'

'She'll be here. Stop worrying about it and kiss me,' he whispered, nibbling at her ear. 'Lord, I think I'll never get enough of you.'

'Stop that!' she muttered against his lips. 'How can she possibly be here for a Christmas wedding? She's in Europe.'

'She'll be here . . . because I've already organised it with her,' Ryan growled. 'Now stop arguing and come here.'

And his lips and hands were controlling her, destroying any further arguments she could possibly have raised. It was much, much later when she finally got round to asking how he'd dared to organise her wedding date without even asking her . . . and by then it didn't really matter.

THE NORTHERN LIGHTS

Many years ago the peoples of the Canadian north thought that on cold clear nights they could see their gods striding magnificently across the heavens. Today we call these apparitions the aurora borealis, or northern lights, which Victoria Gordon mentions in *Battle of Wills*. These dancing sheets of greenish, sometimes reddish light, shimmering like great folds of draperies blowing in a strong wind, fill the entire northern sky, and are especially vivid in late summer and early spring.

The aurora appears in both the far northern and far southern hemispheres (where it is called the aurora australis or southern lights), over an area called the auroral zone, a 300-mile-wide strip of the Earth's surface. In the northern hemisphere, the auroral zone stretches from northern Canada and Greenland around to Iceland and Norway, then on to Northern Siberia and Alaska. The northern lights often reach more than 200 miles into the atmosphere and can be seen up to 700 miles away!

Today, of course, there is a scientific explanation for the aurora, although even scientists haven't cleared up all the mysteries surrounding it. Particles of electronically charged oxygen and hydrogen called "solar wind" strain at great speed toward the Earth from the sun. Scientists believe these particles enter the atmosphere and descend the outstretched magnetic "fingers" projected by the Earth from the auroral zones. The particles from outer space react with the planet's atmosphere, producing a shimmering array of colors in the night sky.

A truly heavenly sight!

Great old favorites...
Harlequin Classic Library

The **HARLEQUIN CLASSIC LIBRARY** is offering some of the best in romance fiction— great old classics from our early publishing lists. Complete and mail this coupon today!

Harlequin Reader Service

In U.S.A. 1440 South Priest Drive
Tempe, AZ 85281

In Canada 649 Ontario Street
Stratford, Ontario N5A 6W2

Please send me the following novels from the Harlequin Classic Library. I am enclosing my check or money order for $1.50 for each novel ordered, plus 75¢ to cover postage and handling. If I order all nine titles at one time, I will receive a FREE book, *Doctor Bill*, by Lucy Agnes Hancock.

- ☐ 109 **Moon over the Alps**
  Essie Summers
- ☐ 110 **Until We Met**
  Anne Weale
- ☐ 111 **Once You Have Found Him**
  Esther Wyndham
- ☐ 112 **The Third in the House**
  Joyce Dingwell

- ☐ 113 **At the Villa Massina**
  Celine Conway
- ☐ 114 **Child Friday**
  Sara Seale
- ☐ 115 **No Silver Spoon**
  Jane Arbor
- ☐ 116 **Sugar Island**
  Jean S. MacLeod

☐ 117 **Ship's Doctor**
Kate Starr

Number of novels checked @ $1.50 each =	$ _____
N.Y. and Ariz. residents add appropriate sales tax	$ _____
Postage and handling	$ .75
TOTAL $	_____

I enclose _____
(Please send check or money order. We cannot be responsible for cash sent through the mail.)

Prices subject to change without notice.

Name _____
(Please Print)

Address _____
(Apt. no.)

City _____

State/Prov. _____ Zip/Postal Code _____

Offer expires July 31, 1983   30456000000

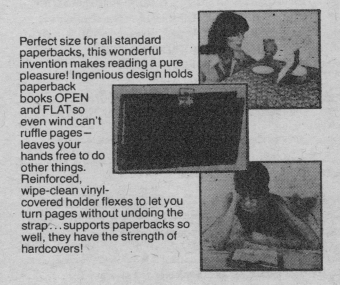

Harlequin Presents

ALL-TIME FAVORITE BESTSELLERS
...love stories that grow more beautiful with time!

Now's your chance to discover the earlier great books in Harlequin Presents, the world's most popular romance-fiction series.

Choose from the following list.

ALL-TIME FAVORITE BESTSELLERS

Complete and mail this coupon today!

- -

Harlequin Reader Service

In the U.S.A.
1440 South Priest Drive
Tempe, AZ 85281

In Canada
649 Ontario Street
Stratford, Ontario N5A 6W2

Please send me the following **ALL-TIME FAVORITE BESTSELLERS.** I am enclosing my check or money order for $1.75 for each copy ordered, plus 75¢ to cover postage and handling.

☐ #17	☐ #35	☐ #41	☐ #66	☐ #73
☐ #20	☐ #36	☐ #42	☐ #67	☐ #75
☐ #29	☐ #38	☐ #50	☐ #70	☐ #78
☐ #32	☐ #39	☐ #62	☐ #71	

Number of copies checked @ $1.75 each = $ _____
N.Y. and Ariz. residents add appropriate sales tax $ _____
Postage and handling $ ___.75
TOTAL $ _____

I enclose _____
(Please send check or money order. We cannot be responsible for cash sent through the mail.)
Prices subject to change without notice.

NAME _____
(Please Print)

ADDRESS _____ APT. NO. _____

CITY _____

STATE/PROV. _____

ZIP/POSTAL CODE _____

Offer expires July 31, 1983   30456000000